MIKE AND JAN, JOHN AND JANET

MIKE AND JAN, JOHN AND JANET

John Evans

Book Guild Publishing

Sussex, England

First published in Great Britain in 2007 by
The Book Guild Ltd
Pavilion View
19 New Road
Brighton BN1 1UF

Typesetting in Baskerville by
SetSystems Ltd, Saffron Walden, Essex

Printed in Great Britain by
CPI Bath

A catalogue record for this book is
available from the British Library

ISBN 978-1-84624-074-4

1

It was in reality quite a depressing situation. His sister had never married, and as far as Mike knew had only ever been out with two men in her 62 years of life, and that had been in her teens. His mother, who had been widowed at 36, had never remarried and seemed to have remained in a perpetual state of mourning. Both had always lived together under the same roof and had developed quite isolationist views on life. They lived their lives through others, sucking life and experiences out of Mike, Janice and their family, as surrogates to their own unfulfilled exsistence, rather like vampires, although Mike would haved shirked from making such a cruel comparison himself. He loved them both and after all was said and done, they were immensely loving and caring people – but, yes, demanding.

As Mike steered the car out into the stream of traffic, Janice seated beside him continued her energetic waves of goodbye. Through the car mirror he could see his mother, now in her eighties, and his sister, still standing at the kerb waving and wearing the expression of mourners at a graveside. And to complete the picture, it was beginning to rain. Once out of sight, Mike and Janice relaxed back into their seats, letting out huge involuntary sighs. Both were equally grateful that the statuary visit had been completed, and to celebrate their release Janice opened up the large bag of mixed sweets that had been thrust upon them as yet another expression of his mother's and sister's concern. It was just as though Mike and Jan were still children. Jan handed Mike an opened Mars bar. Neither of them spoke, it didn't seem necessary. Besides, these visits usually had a nullifying effect on them both.

The car was now out of the town and travelling through what was left of the green belt countryside and heading for the motorway link. Mike was always in a nostalgic mood on these return trips. The act of leaving the town again reminding him more strongly of their original departure from the place of their birth, never more so than when he drove past the entrance to a narrow country lane that led eventually to what used to be a secluded farm. At this point he would smile to himself, remembering those carefree happy school-boy times, his smile broadening further as he also recalled it was the place where, aged eleven or so, he had discovered the wondrous mechanism of masturbation – his five-fingered friend. In those now distant days of his childhood the area had been so rural, even remote. And whenever possible he used to cycle the five miles or so to his schoolfriend's quiet farmstead home, submerging himself into the farming tasks. Often he would stay for weekends and sleep in a little, under the roof room – the room where the marvellous discovery had taken place. Now the town was nearly up to the front door and he felt saddened by the loss of yet one more place of tranquillity.

On this occasion Mike was in an even deeper reminiscing mood than usual and he suspected the onset of the male menopause. Or, he realised, that at 64 years old it was more likely to be the beginnings of senility. But far more possible it was their travels around the hometown that had increased the intensity of his nostalgia. They were now onto the motorway and heading to the rural heartlands of Wales, his eyes staring blankly ahead yet his brain whirred on. Janice, stirring beside him and rummaging in the sweet bag broke his thoughts.

'You're very quiet.' She patted him on the knee as she spoke. 'You're miles away.'

'Umm, oh yeah, I was just thinking how Baray has gone down hill.'

'God, yes. Did you see all that rubbish in the town centre? Don't they have street cleaning any more? Disgusting. And all those closed-up shops, really sad.'

'The place is a mess, Jan. The whole atmosphere has changed somehow. Mind you, we're outsiders now we might see it differently if we still lived there.'

'Uh, I don't think I'd like to live there again. And all those new housing estates. The place is so much bigger now,' Jan retorted, giving a shudder and grimace of distaste.

She became silent again and settled down into her car dozing position, and he slipped back into the past. He agreed with Jan. No, he wouldn't like to live there again. However, the town and many of the people in it used to be so very important to them both.

His mental meanderings on this day had précised his recent impressions of his hometown into an almost lyrical form, and he thought of the town as sitting, or rather slumped, upon its past glories, its triumphant moneymaking coating of coal dust that one time covered large parts of the place, long since washed away. The tattered remnants of its once famous docklands empty and now dotted with small peasant scale industrial enterprises. The massive, wealth-making coal-tipping towers gone, shipped away to other lands, only to be returned as symbols of domestic success – refrigerators, washing machines and Japanese cars. Even the huge plastics factory from which he was made redundant, lay idle. Surrounding fields once green and wooded were now covered with rabbit-hutch homes. What now remained

3

of the older more elegant abodes, looked out at the world through cheap plastic windows and doors. Many were no longer family homes but old people's hospices, or smoke-filled dispensaries of booze. The town centre, once thriving and often filled with foraging sailors, their pockets filled with strange incalculable currencies, now a tawdry run-down mess.

'Christ, you mad bastard,' Mike screeched, as a lorry cut in front of him, chucking up buckets of spray and momentarily obscuring his view.

'What happened, love?' said Janice, stirring from her dozing.

'We're OK. Just a mad trucker.'

The rain, and the Friday evening traffic, was heavy, and he hated driving with the screen wipers flicking back and forth. Mike glanced at his watch and the mileometer, another one and a half hours before reaching home. The driving disturbance over, he once again slipped back into his memories. God, was it really 35 years since they left the town. 1969, that was literally in the last century – how time flies. He thought how strange it was that places, people, and exciting and extraordinary events that once absorbed so much of his and Jan's life, had faded into, well, ordinariness. He supposed that the passage of time was to blame, and that some memories simply wear out. Stranger still, looking at themselves now as grey-haired and arthritic old farts, complete with Janice's disabled badges, was how they had become involved in the town's permissive sexual uprising at all. In fact, Mike often had to remind himself of the power, the passion and excitement of the teenage sexual drive when hearing or reading about teenage behaviour. Their grandchildren, who considered them to be incredibly ancient and old-fashioned, would certainly think such behaviour on their part totally unbelievable.

4

Mike mused that way back then industrial South Wales didn't immediately conjure up images of picturesque beauty nor appear as a likely venue for anything remotely exciting, let alone sexual revolution. Of course it had been the Sixties. But then again, that was a time when marriage and fidelity were still the expected social norm, as indeed it had been for them. Their parents would have been horrified and heartbroken had they just lived together, or if Jan and become pregnant before they were married. And yet they had stepped outside that everyday norm. Mike had often relived, in his head, the people and events they had been involved with, usually with the regret he hadn't been with more women, or at least explored the more sensual and erotic possibilities of his brief relationships with them. In those distant days he was only interested in his own quick satisfaction. Jan must have had similar thoughts but neither of them ever actually talked about what each of them had got up too, or exactly with whom. It was strange, almost as though it had never happened at all.

It would be too pretentious to think that what they did was of any importance to the world at large. Throughout time there have been people that haven't followed the rules so there was nothing new in that aspect of their actions. And after all, ordinary people, in everyday situations, have been more effective than Acts of Parliament in bringing about change, although no doubt one day in the future someone would make a really, really important documentary about how society was changed by behaviour such as his, or Jan's. At the time, they had no such ideas of historical immortality. Their only concern was coping with everyday life and their own conflicting inner needs. But here they were, still together after 40 years.

'If this rain keeps up shall we stop off and have a cuppa?'

'Why not? We can pretend we're on holiday.'

She gave a wry smile and patted his knee again.

'OK OK,' Mike replied, smiling. 'I know it's been a boring day but it isn't very often and Mum is getting on, so I should try to see more of her really.'

'I know, love, I'm only joking,' Jan said. Her own parents were now both dead. 'Usual place?'

'Yep, OK.'

Their usual place was now a very large cafe and petrol complex. But they both remembered it before the motorway came through.

'Do you remember it when it was more like a shed, Darl?'

Darl was their pet name for each other, short for darling.

'God yes, we used to have the kids with us then. It was always full of lorry drivers. It seems ages ago, it was a lot cheaper then, mind you most things were. What made you think of that now?' Jan asked quizzically.

'I don't know. I've been thinking back a lot today.'

'Must be old age.'

'Yes thank you, sweetheart, I've already thought of that one,' Mike said with mock anger.

'What have you been thinking about then?'

'Oh I don't know, the old days, me working in the lab, and what we used to get up to, wife swapping an' that . . .'

Mike knew, even as he spoke what Jan's reaction would be.

'It wasn't wife swapping and that was years ago,' Jan said defensively.'

'Yes, but you know what I mean,' Mike replied and sensed Jan's predicted tetchiness, yet playfully deciding to push his luck. 'I thought I would write it all down. You know, like a book and try and get it published.'

'Don't you dare. I don't want people reading about me. Jan retorted energetically.

Mike smiled to himself. After being married for 40 years they knew each other's reactions pretty damn well. As the car cruised on towards the cafe they slipped once more into the silence of familiarity. He, however, continued to recall the past, wondering if he were to write his memories down, where would he begin . . . ?

2

'What's to eat? I'm in work in a couple of hours.'
'I could do you beans on toast,' she replied meekly.
'Bloody beans on toast, and work all night, you useless bitch.'
He spoke softly but with menace.
'You forgot to give me any money, I haven't been shopping.'
'Give you money, huh, don't be stupid.'
But he really wasn't hungry. Unknown to her he'd stuffed his face with steak and chips in town earlier that afternoon. He simply enjoyed taunting her.

On a still winter night such as this, the factory flare stack burning off waste gases, the lazy billowing clouds of steam and the many well-lit cooling towers were almost welcoming. However, this image was spoilt by the invisible, warm acrid chemical smell that had already permeated the car. If Mike had been a poet he might have called it a satanic miasma or some such – he wasn't, the place stank.

It was a clear cold November night as Mike drove his maroon coloured old Austin A60 through the unlit outskirts of the small Welsh seaside town of Baray towards International Chemicals, Plastics Division. The factory had grown quickly since opening in the late 1940s and was the biggest employer in the area with some 2,500 souls working in the sprawling complex of buildings and pipe work. The shift change over was a busy time and dozens of cars and a couple of works buses were heading in and out through the main gates. And there was much tooting of horns and waves of recognition as Mike parked the car and walked unenthusiastically across the dark unlit car park towards the central control laboratory.

With shoulders hunched against the cold, he wished he were home in bed snuggled up to Janice, but he thought, such is life. The lab, an unimposing flat-roofed building standing on its own, and some way from the processing plant, had no eye-level windows, so even in daylight the place had to be artificially lit, which added to its oppressiveness. As he entered the brightly lit interior he was joined by Crow. Crow was short for his surname Croley. His real name was Robert, but somewhat unbelievably the shift already had two Bobs and so Crow had opted for being – Crow. Being a lanky six-footer with long fair hair and with an easygoing hippy nature, the name really suited him.

'Hi man, how you doing?'

'OK Crow, another bloody night shift.'

'Yeah, last one though, rest days tomorrow – three of 'em – yoh!

'Thank God. Four for me, though I've booked a day off as well,' said Mike cheering up slightly.

'Lucky bugger,' Crow retorted.

'I don't know about that. I'm hoping to finish painting the bathroom.'

'Don't remind me, man, I've got loads to do on my place.'

He got on well with Crow and they often got together as a foursome. In fact, his wife Susan worked as a hairdresser and had cut Mike's hair a couple of times and had given Janice the confidence to do the same. Crow was also doing up an old house so they had plenty in common to talk about. Once inside the building they were hit by the specific chemical odour that pervaded all and even clung to their clothes, which made Janice and the other wives wrinkle their noses with distaste. In the locker room there was the usual babble of incoming and outgoing work mates, each battling for space in the small room, locker doors opening, locker doors slamming shut, eight people trying to get in, eight trying to get out.

'Busy shift boys?' Mike shouted over the mêlée.

'Yeah, six batches going through,' a voice muffled by a jumper over his head replied.

'You'll be busy later,' the voice added.

'Oh great,' muttered Mike, still struggling to don his white lab coat.

Leaving the locker room, he glanced up at the lab clock, and began looking at the analysis reports rowed up on their clipboards at the rostrum desk, and checking the dates were correct.

'November the tenth, nineteen sixty-eight. Twenty two hundred hours, the night begins,' Mike said to himself, but a bit too loudly.

'Talking to yourself? That's a bad sign,' a voice spoke over his shoulder.

It was Roy.

'In this place it's a good sign,' smiled Mike.' How you doing?'

'OK. I'm working on the polyester section tonight.'

'Who's a lucky boy then?' joked Mike.

He hadn't been too sure of Roy at first. He was a stocky chap, podgy faced with immaculate well-greased black hair, the white of his scalp forming a crisp parting. His permanent smirk, which Mike thought had a confident condescending air, didn't really match the voice, which had a strangely nervous tremor to it as though he was frightened of something. Yet he seemed friendly enough and after all it was early days. He had been on the shift for only six weeks and would settle in, and they had already become accustomed to his habit of frequently pushing up his spectacles, which he always wore, over his nose. But as Mike had generously decided, we all have our funny little ways.

The shift camaraderie was important, particularly on the ten-hour night shift. If tempers were to be lost, nine times out of ten the night shift was where it would be. The unnatural hours and fatigue added to the danger of an eruption of emotions, often over trivialities. Luckily enough, most of the eight workers usually worked in separate sections and sometimes would have little contact with each other apart from the tea breaks, and even these were normally staggered because of the workload. Suddenly, the vacuum-operated sample delivery system, similar to the overhead ones in the big local department store, rattled into action and samples from the distant processing plant thudded into the lab.

'Here we go, Crow. The first of the night.'

'Make mine a large one,' joked Crow.

'That's my boy.'

They both laughed and set themselves to the tasks ahead.

At home at the other end of town, Janice was alone watching television. She was used to being on her own at night whilst Mike was a work. In fact, she liked the freedom, although she was rarely idle, and she certainly didn't miss the boring full-time job as a comptometer operator that she had before the children were born. She hadn't really wanted to work in an office and would have liked to have been a hairdresser. And at one time suffered a short-term aberration when she thought of joining the Women's Royal Air Force, just to get away from home. Her parents, however, would hear none of it, and an office job it was. Apart from the children, Mandy aged three and David five, she had many interests. There was the amateur dramatics, acting and singing, making clothes for the kids and helping Mike doing up the house, although she hated housework itself. She was brilliant at solving complex crosswords, read a lot, and now and then did a bit of drawing and painting and was considered by many of her friends to be 'very intelligent' and Mike had often playfully called her a 'smart-arsed grammar school girl'. He was a secondary school boy himself. And now that the youngest was at nursery school for most of the day, she had added a casual daytime barmaid to her itinerary – just for something to do away from the house.

Tonight, however, she was indulging, as she often did, sometimes during the day, in her most secret passion. She lay sprawled over a small sofa and looking at, but not really watching, the television. Her legs were slightly apart, her full-skirted dress was raised up over her knees and, almost absent mindedly, she was touching herself through the thin covering of her knickers Now that the programme was coming to an end she stretched languidly, turned off the television and headed upstairs. As she entered the bedroom Jan was still in the same dreamy mood and feeling especially lustful. Undressing slowly in front of the long dressing mirror, she viewed the body she really didn't like. She hated the baby-scarred belly, the fat she believed she had in abundance. Yet it still excited her to imagine that someone might be secretly watching. Standing watching herself in the mirror, she fondled her full firm breasts, the nipples quickly becoming hard and pert.

Moving to the bed she positioned herself so that she could see herself reflected in the mirror, now with her legs wide apart. Her excitement was building now, her face flushed at the lewdness of her actions. Reaching down between her thighs she gently and slowly parted the vermillion lips, fingers slipping into the warm moistness, her other hand squeezing and lifting her breast to her mouth, her teeth nipping and sucking the pert nipple She continued for sometime looking, feeling, stroking, looking. Her passion was now intense, her breathing heavy. Reaching out for her favourite hand mirror, she watched mesmerised by erotic excitement as with one hand she slid the rounded handle deep inside her, the other hand now frantically rubbing, rubbing, rubbing until, with a breathless gasping screech she came, panting with exertion, pleasure and release. Then slowly, gradually she relaxed, her breathing calming.

Dropping her nightdress over her head, she slid into bed. Before drifting into the deep sleep that usually followed she would often lie thinking, sometimes feeling guilty. Not for the act itself, why should she? After all, she had known, like most people, men and women, this form of pleasure long before 'real sex,' and, unbeknown to her, very many people also keep up the practice for life. In any case, she just wished she could experience such satisfaction with Mike. Jan didn't really like sex with Mike. Not because it was Mike. He was a lovely, gentle, caring person and had been known secretly to snivel at a sad film or the like, but she did think sometimes that perhaps her dissatisfaction was his fault not hers. Then again, perhaps it would be the same with any man. She hated her frustration and the sticky mess that ensued from intercourse. Hated it more because she got nothing out of it. His satisfaction seemed guaranteed. Her attitude to her body hadn't been improved by the troublesome pregnancy with David. She had been in and out of hospital, and so many doctors had prodded and probed that she came to believe her vagina was state property and didn't belong to her. This experience had consolidated the introversion of her sexuality and she had decided she just wanted to control her own body, her own sexuality, by and with herself.

'Our marriage would be great if it wasn't for sex, and he wants so much of it.'

Jan wondered if it was the same for other women,

though she doubted it. She believed that, she, Janice, was the odd one. It wasn't that she didn't like men as such, she did.

'Perhaps I'm queer, a lesbian or something, she mused sleepily, 'or perhaps if I did it with another man it might be different. I don't want to lose Mike.'

She felt safe with him and sheltered somehow from the outside world.

Her eyelids closed and she let out a relaxing sigh.

'Mum, I don't feel very well,' one of the children wailed from their room.

Jan let out another sort of sigh and got out of bed . . .

It was 3.00 a.m. Break time, and some of the shift were in the rest room munching, drinking coffee or tea, and smoking.

'Cecil's noisy tonight,' Mike said in a matter-of-fact manner.

'Perhaps he's on a promise, lucky bugger. ' Crow added in equally matter of fact way, unpacking his snack box and spreading out the contents on the table.

'Could be I suppose and, yeah, I know what you mean, mate,' Mike said lighting up a fag.

'Who the hell is Cecil?' Roy asked quizzically.

Mike and Crow grinned at each other pleased that their unrehearsed double act had had the desired effect of arousing the newcomer's, interest.

'Our resident house cricket. That's what that sort of chirping noise is.'

'I thought it was the heating pipes vibrating or something. I've never heard of a house cricket.'

'It's a bit like a grasshopper, loves the heat of this place, and lives amongst all the pipework. Mind you, no one has ever seen them. They come out at night. How they know the difference in this place I don't know.'

Roy's interest in the subject had already faded and he completely changed the subject.

'Have you read these letters in this mag about wife swapping, Mike? Roy asked.

'I'll have a new car for mine,' said Bill, dryly puffing on his pipe.

They all laughed at this except Roy, who hadn't ever been seen to give a real open-mouthed laugh, he just gave that superior grin of his. Bill, a phlegmatic, moustached and portly chap in his fifties who was the oldest of the group and nicknamed affectionately, and when he wasn't listening, as Old Navy Bill – he'd been a Petty Officer in the Royal Navy, and was a calming influence on the shift's 'youngsters'.

'I bet you still get your leg over,' retorted Crow still laughing.

'That's all you youngsters think of is sex. I need a fortnight's notice now, in writing, before that sort of thing,' replied Bill.

More laughter ensued and Roy, giving up hope of getting Mike's attention, passed the magazine over to him. Mike opened the girly magazine, looking at the naked female bodies as he searched for the letter in question.

Finding the readers' letter page, he scanned some of the other offerings.

'It says here that a man's testosterone levels are the highest at three in the morning. Fat lot of good that is, we're either sleeping or in this place, 'Mike said in some-what incredulous tone.

'Yeah,' agreed Crow and added, 'mind you, it explains that lump in your trousers when we're on night shift.'

They all laughed with enthusiasm.

'Yeah yeah, very good, Crow, and here's another one. There's a couple here that do it twice a day. Twice a year would be more like it,' Mike said adding ruefully, 'I bet he's not a shift worker.'

There were mutterings of good-hearted agreement from the others.

'What we should have is more than one wife. Like those foreign bods, you know the ones with the harems or whatever they're called,' Crow quipped.

'Huh, what?' exclaimed Mike with a tinge of horror in his voice. 'With our luck they would all have headaches at the same time.'

More giggles ensued from the gathering.

'Have you found it yet?' enquired Roy, who was not finding the conversation to his liking.

'Yep, got it.'

'What do you think?'

'Is this for real? I can't see normal couples doing this. Where did all this start anyway? Chucking keys on a table and taking potluck. I'd like to choose.'

'California I think,' chipped in one of the Bobs.

'I might have known – mad Yanks,' said Mike.

'Sounds like a bloody good idea to me, man, 'a change is as good as a rest after all, as the bishop said to the actress,' replied Crow laughingly.

At 19 he was the youngest of the group and the most overtly and recognisably unconventional and he had only got married because Susan was pregnant – and her parents well off.

The group fell quiet once more and each stepped back onto their own planet. Mike carried on reading the girly magazine and gazing at the girls showing all, well not quite all. Pubic hair and that area itself wasn't allowed to be seen, unless of course it was an illegal foreign magazine. He read not because he needed the stimulation, far from it, he already had a big sexual appetite. He read the letters page and perused the pictures because he was sexually curious, particularly since he had married and, anyway, 'knowledge is power' as one of his schoolteachers had often instilled. He was by nature a thinker, an analyser, a planner, but cheerful with it; in fact, his mind did it on its own and was always busy with thoughts of life, love, sex and the ethics of various ideas. Jan wasn't a deep thinker and admitted as much. She hated confrontation and preferred to keep a low profile, letting issues take their natural course, not really considering what that natural course might be. And she would often be mildly irked by Mike's endless planning and written 'lists of jobs' he had to do around the house.

Slowly, or so it seemed, the shift dragged to an end. Everyone dispersed home to live their own lives, for a few days at least. Driving back home, Mike felt happy and relaxed, smoking an unrushed cigarette as he made his way through the awakening town. He was a happy, optimistic person, more so when he thought of having time to do his own thing, and the night-time reading of the sex magazines had also heightened his desire for sex. He parked the car on the street outside the house and he was soon unlocking the front door and greeting the children, who were already dressed and heading out to school.

'Hi, kiddie winks. Off already?'

'Rita said she'd take them in for me today,' Jan answered.

Rita was a neighbour from a few doors down the terrace. She was a rotund, jolly person, and had two kids of her own, but she was always ready to help Jan out.

'Oh great, see you upstairs then,' he said with a lecherous grin and giving Jan a quick kiss on the cheek.

Jan said nothing and briskly turned away and fussed with the children's coats.

'I promised I would help her making some curtains.'

'There's no rush is there?'

'I said I'd be there by nine thirty.'

'That loads of time.'

Jan quickly added,' And I want to pop down town to the shops first. Now that you're home I can use the car.'

'That's a bloody nice welcome. I might as well get to bed,' Mike muttered, uncharacteristically showing how peeved he was.

'Don't be like that, Mike.'

Mike was already on his way up the stairs, muttering, 'Oh sod off,' under his breath as he did so.

'What the hell is she doing for sex?' Mike thought bitterly. Not much point in being married. It's months since we did it. Is it another man? No, not Jan. But how can she do without it for so long? He believed all women wanted sex, just as men did. Jan's attitude was a mystery to him.

Mike reached the bedroom, throwing off his jacket and other clothes anywhere to hand. As he did so the magazine he had been looking at in work fell out of the jacket pocket. He had brought it home, as he often did, for Jan to look at, hoping it might inspire an interest in sex. As he climbed into the bed he revelled in the warmth of Jan's body that it still retained. He had calmed down now and began to relax, picking up the magazine and looking at the pictures once again and felt that at least he was in the company of women. Bringing home books and photos from work was becoming a familiar practice for him of late. Jan's lack of amorous intent had reawakened his enthusiasm for his five-fingered friend, although for him the opportunity for such private entertainment was thin on the ground. Jan, and doubtless other housewives, were luckier because for much of their time they had the house to themselves.

The comfort of the bed, the prospect of time off from work, the pictures, all assisted the burgeoning erection. God, I wish Jan were here, he thought, touching himself and feeling the now hard warmth between his legs. Stroking lightly, he teased himself, building the excitement until he could no longer resist the pulsating urgency he felt. His hand closed more firmly around the throbbing pleasure. His hand moving ever more quickly – then in frantically faster movements, his hips involuntarily thrusting up and down as he climaxed with a deep, loud, satisfied grunt.

3

'It's two o'clock Darl – here's coffee,' said Janice cheerfully, drawing open the bedroom curtains as she spoke.

That morning's tiff was, as usual, being glossed over by Janice who simply wanted a peaceful unpressured existence. But for Mike the issue was of greater importance and not so easily forgotten and her bright avoidance of the issue annoyed him. They very rarely rowed, in fact perhaps only once or twice since their marriage, and even then they were very low-key events and usually quickly mended. But these fractious events had become more and more frequent and had sneakily eroded the closeness they once enjoyed.

'Uh yeah, right,' slurred Mike, dragging himself back to consciousness. It seemed to him that he had only just gone to sleep. 'I'm shattered.'

'It's a lovely afternoon, sunny,' Janice said breezily as she busied herself tidying up his clothes, which were strewn over a floral-patterned linen chest.

'Phew, that smell of the factory – on these clothes – it's awful, and you shouldn't bring your jacket up here, it stinks of that place,' said Jan, holding the clothes well away from her, and dropping them disdainfully into the laundry basket.

'Do you want to sleep on? You said to wake you at two.'

'No, no, it's OK. I won't sleep tonight if I don't wake up now.'

His eyes felt full of gravel as he blinked against the

sunlight now streaming into room. The changeover from the gruelling seven-day, ten-hour night shifts to the three-day rest period were always hard. Even more so in the summer when, with all that daylight about he seemed to be missing out on so much life. Many of the other members of his shift felt the same, which was yet another bonding factor with his colleagues. Not that the work was physically hard as such. With a posh title of technical assistant grade five, one might be forgiven for thinking it was a cushy job. But the hours were long and the job needed precision and concentration.

Mike drank his coffee and soon the urge for a cigarette surfaced. He would have to get up soon – they never smoked in the bedroom. His mind was fuzzy, numb almost, and his stomach felt raw as though he had been vomiting. The strange and unpleasant feeling reminded him how he hated shift work, but it did pay very well, nearly £900 a year. Mike had previously tried his hand as a self-employed landscape gardener, and still did some paid work for some of his previous customers. However, the money had been slow coming in and irregular and after the birth of their first child, David, it soon became obvious that more money and a house were needed. The flat that they had started out married life in was totally inadequate.

'And what are you going to do today, Mike? Painting?' said Janice, completing her tidying and her voice breaking through his befuddlement.

'Um yes. I thought I'd finish the bathroom and perhaps tomorrow tidy up the garden a bit.'

Garden, huh that's a laugh, Mike reflected sadly. Several square yards of rubbish created from his DIY. He missed the large expanse of his mother's garden that he used to tend before getting married. Mike enjoyed gardening, in fact after leaving school at 15 he had gone to work in the local council parks' department and then at 16 on to a horticultural college, a fact that Jan resented a little, jealous of his parents encouraging him to leave home and supporting him for a year to study what interested him – something her parents hadn't done for her. He would have liked to been a plant pathologist and after leaving college had studied for 'O' and 'A' levels to get a university entrance. However, with the death of his father his mother hinted strongly that he should get a job to help out with the household money. He got the 'Os' and tried to study the 'A' level subjects in evening classes but this proved to be difficult, in fact impossible when on shift work and this had been a big disappointment for him.

'Good idea, though the kids will miss the heaps of bricks and stuff. Still they might stay cleaner.'

'Mm, this coffees good, should help my brain to work.'

'I'll go down then. What do you want to eat?'

'Not a lot, Darl,' Mike said cheerfully, ever hopeful that his cheerfulness would lead to resumption of normal bedroom activity. He stretched and yawned noisily, 'I'll wait until later.'

'OK shall I take the cup?'

'Yeah, thanks.'

Later, when his mind felt strong enough to cope with the real world, including the boisterous children screeching in the rear garden, Mike got dressed and made his way downstairs.

'I thought you'd gone back to sleep.'

'As if I would.'

He smiled. Yes, he was feeling better he told himself. Lighting up a cigarette, Mike sat down at the table, which still bore the remains of the kids' lunch, dishes besmeared with tomato sauce, a couple of lonely baked beans and partly chewed and discarded pieces of bread and butter.

Janice was busy in the kitchen peeling potatoes for the evening meal.

'By the way, there's a drama do tonight,' Jan said with voice raised.

'Oh God no,' Mike said under his breath.

He was not an avid partygoer; they seemed so purposeless but knew that when he did make the effort to go, and had a few drinks, he would probably feel differently.

'You don't have to come,' said Janice in joking tone, reading his silence as his reticence.

'You can stay and look after the kids. Cheaper than paying the baby sitter.'

Jan came in from the kitchen. They smiled at each other, and Janice bent to give Mike a quick kiss.

'Sure you don't want something to eat?'

'I'll just have a piece of your delicious cake and another cup of coffee.'

'You and your coffee – it's not good for you.'

'Rubbish – shift workers couldn't survive without it.'

'Daddy, Daddy.'

The children erupted into the room.

'Hello hello,' laughed Mike, pleased to see them.

'And what have you two little terrors been up to?'

Later that afternoon, with the children watching television, Mike and Janice inspected the finished bathroom.

'Looks great, love, cooed Jan. 'I'll put the curtains up tomorrow.'

'Pretty good I must say – it's a shame it's a downstairs bathroom though, not really convenient, with the kids.'

'It's fine. Lots of people have downstairs bathrooms – it's better than taking up one of the bedrooms. Anyway, you've put in an upstairs toilet as well – that's really useful for the kids. Well, all of us really.'

'Yeah, that's true, it does look good though,' said Mike, stepping back a bit and reflecting upon all his hard work.

It was a huge improvement on the old tiny bathroom and he was justly proud of his amateur building skills. Jan's dad, who was a bit of a father substitute for Mike, lived a few miles away close to the dockyard where he worked and was a good handyman and had given him lots of building tips. The house, an old three-bedroomed terraced house with no front garden, was situated on a busy road at the edge of a run down area of the town. At one end of the terrace of 12 houses stood a disused shop, at the other a small garage. To complete the scenic view, opposite the row was a redundant towering brick-built incinerator chimney, a council yard and an open air Victorian walk-in gents' urinal. The house itself had needed a lot of work but was now nearing completion. Perhaps later they would move on to a better house, in a better part of town, or buy a caravan, or take the kids on holiday. Meanwhile, however, he would soon have spare time on his hands.

'Will we be able to use it tonight?'

'The paint should be dry. I'll tell you what – why don't we have an open day, invite the neighbours to a bath night – all romping in the nude,' Mike said enthusiastically, taking hold of Janice by the waist.

Janice smiled but he noticed her eyes cloud over at the mention of nudity and sex and she looked away. This reaction of hers had steadily become more frequent over the last 12 months or so. Not that she ever was tremendously enthusiastic and any suggestions of Mike's as to different positions or heaven forbid, oral sex, which Mike had read about and would like to tried, she considered heinous perversities. True, they had been married for six years and were out of the passionate love bite stage, but even so at 26 years for him and 24 years of age for Janice they were far from being 'past it'. Shift work didn't help either. It was difficult forming a pattern for a marital sex life when you were working irregular hours – and had children. Mind you, it seemed to Mike, and many of his married pals, that

24

shift work or not it was always a mystery as to know when was the 'right' time. It's an odd business.

'Come on, sex manic,' Janice said cheerfully, 'let's eat. We're going out tonight, remember?'

Mike groaned, 'Oh yes, I'd forgotten.'

He would have preferred a drink or two at home, an early night, and a long overdue loving session with Jan. Still, perhaps the night out would be stimulating.

With the children fed, washed and ready for bed and now re-glued to the television, Mike and Janice were free to prepare themselves.

'Let's have a bath together – to christen it,' he suggested with a smirk.

To his surprise, she agreed and once in the bath Mike gazed with familiar rapture at Jan's body glistening with remnants of soap and water. Mike reached out, touching silky smooth breasts, his fingertips gently brushing over the large pink nipples; he thought she was incredibly desirable. Whenever he told Jan as much, she would laugh saying that she was too fat, too short – she really didn't think she was anything but plain. True, she wasn't tall, some five feet three, not slim but not fat and he thought she was perfect.

She had dark hair, dark hair, bordering on black and swept back into what she called, much to Mike's amusement, a 'French roll,' dark blue eyes, and a lovely rounded face. And he knew from comments from other men that she was far from plain, and her teeth and mouth, he had a thing about this, were again perfect. On one occasion, when he was about 16, he had been travelling on a bus and found a girl's mouth and teeth shape, the movements of her naked uncoloured lips as she spoke to her friends, so spellbinding that he had stared so intently and for too long that the girl moved to another part of the bus.

However, Mike had never critically compared Jan's body

with other women. He had never been with other women; Janice had been the first. It had been the same for Jan. Of course, as in all male work places there were always plenty of images of naked females for comparison, in books, magazines, even eight millimetre blue films all readily available, particularly during the night shifts. However, for Mike the differences in women's bodies were to be relished not standardised.

'We haven't time for that now,' Janice said in a relaxed dreamy voice – and smiled.

He was pleased with her reaction – at least she smiled. Her attitude to sex was a problem to him. Whenever they did actually make love it seemed to Mike that she seemed to enjoy it well enough. It was her inconsistency and reluctance – the constant need for him to make all the moves that Mike found puzzling. It was as though she was constantly applying the brakes to her sexual feelings. But why? They were so very close in all other aspects – they were happy – laughed a lot, well used to . . .

'Come on, Darl, we had better get going, we're going to be late, the baby sitter will be here soon.'

Mike watched her get out of the bath, as she did so his eyes searched, hoping for a glimpse of her exposed secret pink folds beneath the dark pubic hair. His salacious thoughts and the mammary stroking had produced the beginnings of a healthy erection. As he stood and stepped out of the bath, Janice laughed.

'And you can put that thing away,' she said, giving Mike a playful flick of the towel as she headed to the bedroom to dress.

4

The party, actually just a get together to discuss the next production, was being held at the community hall, a grand title for a glorified shack, clad with corrugated iron and set in a patch of overgrown grass. It had a small stage and some tiny dressing rooms and was used by the Baray Drama and Musical Society as a venue for lesser productions and also for smaller social dos. Mike considered the place to have one major advantage – it was informal. There was no sense in wearing ultra tidy clothes, he wasn't one for dressing formally anyway, because the old place was rather dusty and had that old musty smell which Mike found quite pleasant. After parking the car they went inside to find the place already quite full, which was unusual as most people tanked up in the nearby pub before entering the portals later in the evening.

'Hi Jan, oh, and Mike as well – not working?'

A dark-haired, olive-skinned girl, tall, gawky and with a largish Roman nose greeted them both.

'No – I'm yours for the night,' Mike replied, waving the bottle of wine he'd brought at her. 'As long as your big hairy gun-toting boyfriend isn't around.'

'He doesn't change does he?' laughed Marie.

Marie worked for some sort of advertising agency, and could often be seen around the town centre offering free cigarettes one day, or packets of soap on another. Marie and Janice went off discussing some inconsequential point or other in earnest and conspiratorial tones, leaving Mike to search for a bottle opener.

Most of the men involved in this drama thing were not Mike's type at all – they probably didn't like him either. They tended to be rather pretentious, not at all down to earth. Mike tolerated some of the least affected types like Bill for instance – the world seemed full of Bills and Bobs. A dapper chap in his forties with greying hair, older than most of the other men, and quietly spoken, which was rare for an insurance salesman, He was in fact the big chief of the 'am dram' set and despite his quiet manner produced and directed many of the shows. But generally Mike preferred chatting with the females. He enjoyed flirting with them, gauging their reactions and estimating how far they would be willing to go. It exercised his mind. It seemed a safe enough pastime as he didn't consider he was any sort of Adonis to whom women would succumb, swooning at his feet. His longish face, the slightly lopsided smile, the lanky five foot ten body topped with a mass of curly fair hair, not forgetting the rather prominent ears, although these were fairly well hidden under the hair, all amounted to a very average appearance. But he had very nice blue eyes and boyish good looks as Jan, once upon a time, would remind him.

Mike could not understand why people wanted to be in plays and the like. To be someone else and have to learn all those lines seemed hard work. And they all were incredibly nervous before they performed, or so they said, Jan certainly was; yet they all still wanted the biggest part as possible. It seemed extraordinary and a little mad. He supposed some people wanted to be someone else; and of course there was the applause, the recognition of success as a person even if you were pretending to be someone else. Mike thought the other more truthful purpose of joining the group was the opportunity for affairs. After all, the real stars of the cinema and the stage like, Liz Taylor and Zsa Zsa Gabor seemed to be changing husbands on a regular basis and were constantly in the news. And from his infrequent observations of the members this was highly likely amongst this group as well, probably more so when people were in roles that involved kissing and the like. He had sometimes noted surreptitious hand squeezing and intense glances between those he knew to be married to others. He had mentioned this theory to Jan who said his idea was a bit simplistic but didn't dismiss it altogether, and agreed a few members were 'messing about' as she put it, but considered such behaviour to be a rare exception. In any event Mike, remained adamant the whole acting business was to him a bit unreal – 'a bit of the unnecessary' as his grandmother used to say.

Janice was by now well installed amongst her pals and he was left somewhat out in the cold. He found little interest in the drama chat and so drifted about from group to group, gradually becoming less steady as the clutched bottle emptied. One of his meanderings led him close to the entrance and to his surprise he saw Roy, from work, coming in with a woman he presumed to be his wife. Despite his poor eyesight, he wore very thick lenses; Roy made a beeline for Mike, almost dragging the woman behind him.

'Hello, Mike, didn't expect to see you here.'

'Nor me, Roy. You're late, aren't you?'

'We've been in the pub, you look as though you've had a few as well, and . . . this is Barbara, the missus.'

'The missus? Oh right – your wife. Hello.'

Mike kissed her hand. The booze was working now. She giggled awkwardly, but Roy seemed strangely pleased.

'I'll leave you two then, I want to have a word with Peter for a minute.'

'Right, Roy I'll take good care of her,' Mike said putting his arm around Barbara and leading her to a seat.

'Do you want a drink? I didn't know that Roy was interested in this drama lark.'

She refused a drink and added, 'Well he's only just joined.'

'And you?'

'Oh no, I've got the kids to see to, we can't both go out.'

'Oh right, I see.'

He didn't really see at all. Hadn't she heard of baby sitters?

Mike found himself already liking Barbara. She had a slim figure, pretty light brown eyes and her mousy-coloured short hair was somewhat disarrayed and even to Mike's fashionless eye, her skirt and jumper had seen better days. She seemed very natural, and sort of schoolgirlishly, grinned a lot, in a nervous way, and acted rather coyly. And as she chatted he noticed she had an interesting mouth and teeth, and couldn't actually be so young as she had two little girls at home. She seemed overawed that he was bothering to talk to her at all. As for Mike, as his alcoholic euphoria increased he began to behave rather physically towards her, laughingly kissing his way up her arms and kissing her neck. Barbara was totally bemused by the whole business but didn't move away. Mike wasn't usually quite so flamboyant in his actions but on this occasion it just seemed so, well, easy.

The evening moved on and someone had brought in a record player and set it up on the stage where Mary Hopkins was belting out her latest hit, 'Those Were The Days', and also the inevitable long-running Beatles' 'Hey Jude' and a few people were dancing about rather half-heartedly on the small stage and the overall sound level had reached that familiar party pitch. Eventually Roy returned.

'Having fun?' he said jovially, well, as jovial as he ever got, and he didn't seem at all bothered by Mike's antics with his wife.

30

'Yeah yeah, good night, yeah. Wanna a smoke?' Mike asked, attempting to light the wrong end of his tipped cigarette.

'Do you know Pete then?' Mike went on, offering the packet to Roy and Barbara.

'Barbara does, don't you love? He's been to the house a couple of times.'

'Wiring job was it? He's a good electrician.'

'Not really. We live in a flat in Harbour Side Road, I don't have to do any repairs.'

Mike was impressed. Harbour Side Road overlooked cliff-top Municipal Gardens and an old silted up harbour – very picturesque. And the houses were late Victorian, large three-storey abodes – very pricey. Rents would be high perhaps as much as three or four pounds a week and Mike hazily wondered how Roy could afford it.

'Actually, we had a threesome – you know, three in a bed.'

He spoke in that controlled, shaky nervous tone he had.

'Oh yeah, right,' said Mike disbelievingly and thinking this must be his idea of a joke.

Barbara had fallen silent and sat hunched as through she was trying to disappear into the floor. Roy carried on in his quiet matter-of-fact manner, ignoring her obvious discomfort.

'You know a bit about cameras don't you, Mike?'

'I've done a bit, developing, printing and stuff like that.'

' 'Cos I'm thinking of getting one of these new Polaroid cameras.'

Mike wasn't really up to concentrating on real issues. He was comfortable, relaxed. He didn't want to be sober, to make the effort – but did.

'Yeah, really clever gadgets, only black and white pictures though. Isn't the film a bit expensive?'

' 'Tis a bit, about one and sixpence a print, but it's only

for special photos – know what I mean? I can't take our sort of films to a shop. Can I, love, eh?'

He directed the latter remark to Barbara who gave a weak giggle but hardly lifted her head.

'Anyway, when I get it, you can have a look at it and you – and Janice, must come over – for a drink or something. You can give me a ring if you like, we're on the 'phone.'

He gave one of his lip-curled sneers and looked at Mike over the top of his glasses with piggy-like brown eyes. Before Mike could make any further comment, such as he wasn't, 'on the 'phone,' Jan and Marie, still talking enthusiastically, returned from the inner sanctum of the am dram, actually a scruffy side room where Supremo Bill had been doling out the parts for the new show.

'Hi, Jan, having fun?' Mike said with a grin and a wave.

'You have. We've been watching you,' said Marie with a laugh, obviously referring to his antics with Barbara.

Janice, however, was rather cooler towards his behaviour, but tried not to let it show.

'Time to go,' shouted a voice.

It was the caretaker, an old wizened little fellow who always had a fag between his quivering thin blue lips even when he spoke, and whenever he did so showers of grey ash would be sent in all directions, mostly over his tattered woollen jumper. In his cloudy mind Mike considered what an interesting but usually anonymous lot caretakers were. Many had had other careers and were just filling in time. Many had useful attributes and the one in the lab, for instance, supplied the shifts with blue films and books. It was only 11.30 p.m. but this particular caretaker's word was the law and revellers had already begun heading towards the door.

'It's time we went, Barbara,' said Roy and she instantly stood up.

'Yeah,' said Mike, 'we have to be out by midnight otherwise we'll all change into pumpkins or something.'

'You've had to much to drink – I'll drive,' Jan said and held out her hand.

'Me? Never,' said Mike laughing, in truth more fatigued than drunk.

After all, he'd only had about five and a half hours' sleep. He fumbled for the keys, handing them to Janice.

'Bye Marie, bye bye, Babs,' Mike said, grinning idiotically, 'see you sometime.'

'See you in work, Mike,' Roy said as he waved.

'Don't remind me,' said Mike, giving a mock vomit of disgust.

Janice was in a happy and animated mood as she drove homeward, pleased that she had been given a leading singing role in the next production, which was to be *The Desert Song*. It was originally a 30s' musical hit, and was to be staged in the large local theatre, so for the group it was to be a very big production indeed. It would mean lots of rehearsals and lots of baby sitting for Mike, which was not a problem as they had long ago agreed to support each other's interests. In fact, Mike thought Jan was brilliant at that sort of thing and he got great personal pride and kudos from her public appearances. He hadn't always had this view. Before he meet Jan he had the unusual idea that musical shows, pop songs even dancing were all frivolous, pretentious and unintelligent rubbish. Perhaps his deeply innate feelings of inadequacy made him, in a way, jealous of those who could don make-up and appear in front of an audience. After all, he was as much of a frustrated extrovert trying to be a real one as Janice was an introvert wishing to be an extrovert.

The journey was cheerful enough although there were one or two sour notes. One was Jan's curt comments about his enthusiastic playtime with Barbara, the other, her opinion of Roy, who, it seemed, had introduced himself to her whilst on his way to find Peter, as 'a bit creepy and slimy'. To which Mike, had to some extent, drunkenly contested.

'And why did you have to mention that gun-toting nonsense to Marie?'

'No harm in that was there? Everybody knows about him anyway. I was only joking – didn't seem to bother Marie. Anyway, I wouldn't like to get on the wrong side of him and meet him in a dark alley – he'd scare the manure out of me.'

He giggled drunkenly at his witty euphemism.

Marie's boyfriend had only recently come to Wales from somewhere in the rural North of England, apparently after he had been accused of threatening behaviour with a shotgun – nice bloke. He never came to the am dram and Mike had only ever seen him once with Marie when Mike and Jan had been shopping in the town centre. They both found him a rather intimidating character. He was big chunky bloke with an unruly bushy beard, staring eyes and didn't seem to work yet looked prosperous. They thought that perhaps he might be a bit of a crook. Anyway, Marie seemed to think he was a God on wheels.

In any event Jan ignored his comments and carried on talking about Barbara.

'She was in the grammar school with me, a class down I think. She's a bit younger than me. You know who her parents are, don't you?'

'No idea,' slurred Mike.

'Well, you know that night club sort of place by the old harbour, 66 Sunset Club or something like that – well, her parents run it. They must be loaded, it's packed nearly every night. Mind you, they're big churchgoers, which is a bit odd seeing what they do for a living.'

34

Mike wondered how Jan knew so much about it but didn't have the energy to enquire.

'66 Sunset Club. Perhaps it's a strip club. You know, *66 Sunset Strip* – the programme on TV.'

'Don't be silly, it's not that sort of club,' Jan retorted, 'and it's *77 Sunset Strip*.'

'What is?'

'The programme on television, it's *77 Sunset Strip*, and they're detectives not strippers,' Jan said with exasperation.

'Well, Roy was going on about wife-swapping and I thought perhaps Barbara was a stripper or something. He reckons Pete has been swapping with them.'

'You're drunk – in any case, Pete isn't married and I certainly can't see any women wanting to go with Roy, he's odd.'

With that and a dismissive sigh Janice brought the conversation to an end.

Some people say that they think best when surrounded by everyday noise and activity. Mike did not. His analysing mode worked best when such distractions were removed, which is why he liked that time before sleep when all is quiet, the eyes not seeing, and the body not asking for earthly attention. It was also why he enjoyed taking the kids out to the countryside on photographing expeditions and also why he liked working in gardens, all such places could be good daytime thinking places and in bed that night after the drama do, his brain began its task of reworking the evening's events.

Mike's most pressing cranial machinations were concerned with Roy's remarks about threesomes. Was he joking? He wondered if Peter had really been involved. He wasn't married so strictly speaking it wouldn't have been a swap – but did that matter? Was the invitation for them to 'drop in' an invitation to a wife swap, like in the magazine?

He didn't think he was much of a joker. In fact, he had seen another side of Roy. His tremulous voice wasn't through lack of confidence and in a social setting he seemed very confident. Babs certainly obeyed him quickly enough but Mike concluded that perhaps she was just in awe of her masterful husband. And what about her reactions when he talked of 'three in bed', she had looked so uneasy. On the other hand, perhaps she likes that sort of thing but doesn't want to broadcast it all over town. After all, she is a married woman with two kids and seems so ordinary, perhaps people might think she was a slut. But there again, what makes someone extraordinary? And then there was Roy talking about their 'threesomes' to a comparative stranger. True or not it was little wonder she seemed so embarrassed.

He wasn't sure he would want to get involved at all – but there again, part of him did. He certainly wouldn't mind going with Barbara. It would be very odd though, so extraordinary, having sex with someone else's wife – with their own wife doing the same with another man. How the hell did it all work? A secret affair he could understand but this didn't seem quite right – bloody exciting though, and what about Jan? She certainly wouldn't want to go with Roy, not the way she felt about him. In fact, it would be very unlikely she would have any interest at all, considering she was off sex. Again he pondered, how does it all work? Of course, on the other hand, if everyone is married then surely it's simpler, everyone just goes home afterward, it's just sex. He wondered how he would feel about Jan having sex with another man. He supposed that if he knew about it, was there in the same room, then that wouldn't be so bad. An affair isn't the same, as sex – is it? Surely affairs lead to break-ups but just sex on its own is OK, isn't it? He had no real ideas as to what could go wrong but sensed lots of thing could. It's all too complicated, he sighed we'll just carry on as we are, things aren't so bad really and there's always the five-fingered friend to fall back on. Not very manly but better than nothing. What is the difference anyway between love and sex? God, losing Jan and our way of life would be a bloody disaster. It's not worth the risk. We're OK, really – Mike's mind was scribbling now, losing clarity. Sleep was slithering into his brain cells and soon he was asleep.

5

Mike's mother lived in an area that she liked to call the 'West end' of town. The west end was considered the best part of the town but actually his mother's house was a mile or so away from it, and close to the small council estate where Mike had lived until he was 18 and before Mike's grandfather had left this house to his mother.

Nevertheless the row of 1930s' large, bay-windowed terraced houses stood in a very pleasant elevated spot with a middle distant view of the docks and the large sandy bay, and with sizable gardens to the front and rear. In contrast, Jan's parents lived in a tiny terraced house close to where the coal tipping into cargo ships took place. In fact, their house could just about be seen from the upstairs windows of his mum's. On some days the wind would carry the black dust into the house and Jan's mother could be guaranteed to have a duster in her hands. She was very house proud, and apart from the perpetual dusting she also had the habit of plumping up cushions as soon as you got up, which Mike found a little disconcerting.

Mike and Janice often killed two birds with one stone by collecting the kids from their Welsh-medium school, which was in the 'West' end of town, and calling on his mother.

'Well, what a lovely surprise. Hello, son, Jan and, oh, my little darlings.' In between her words of greeting she busily bestowed kisses upon them all.

'Come in then. I've got a man putting in an extra power point in the kitchen,' she added,' let's see if I can find some sweeties shall I?'

She temporarily ignored Mike and Jan and left them to close the front door behind them and concentrated all her attention upon spoiling the children.

'Sis in work, Mum?' Mike asked, knowing it was a silly question because she worked nine to five and it was only 3.30 p.m. Mum gave an equally obvious answer.

'Yes, love, she'll be home later.'

His unmarried sister, Marion, was a couple of years younger than Mike and worked at the same plastics' factory, but in the research department. Strangely, their paths never crossed at work.

'Cup of coffee?'

'Yes, please, Mum,' said Jan, answering for them both.

'I could have put the power point in for you, Mum. Why didn't you say?'

'Oh no, love, it's all right. You've got enough to do, what with work and doing the house up.'

Actually, Mike really didn't mind not being asked to do the work. Electricity wasn't his strong point. In fact, he had a very healthy respect for it since he was ten years old. He had had a hefty shock when bird nesting with a gang of school friends in an old wartime army camp that used to be situated close to the docks. The building was a huge iron-framed shed and he had touched a bare wire and fallen quite a long way down to the floor. His back had hurt for days and he still feared that horrible, tingling sensation of the electric shock itself. But he never told his parents because the docks area had been out of bounds so, of course, he shouldn't have been there.

'Should she be in a dress in this cold weather, Janice?' Mum asked questioningly.

'She's fine, Mum,' replied Janice through somewhat grit-
ted teeth.

Mike, sensing what was going through Jan's mind,
decided to volunteer to put the kettle on.

'I'll go and put the kettle on, shall I?'

He didn't wait for an answer but headed for the kitchen.

His father had died of cancer when he was 16 years old
and his mother had never remarried. They had been a very
close family and Mike had spent many hours with his father
gardening around the house or on the allotment, and he
still missed him immensely. His mother, a tall, strong-
looking women in her early forties with a oval flattish face
and dull blue, black rimmed eyes looked much older and
her dark dyed hair was always in a fixed curly state. She was
in an understated way a bit of a snob, and Mike could still
remember the day his mother suddenly announced that
the 'lav' was henceforth to be called the toilet, and dessert forks appeared alongside the familiar dessert spoons.
Appearances both physical and social were of huge importance to her and she would never be seen without the
regulation make-up. As regards to the social aspect, she had
a knack of bending Mike, Jan and Marion to her social
model, with a mixture of close to sobbing cajolery and
unyielding insistence – a lethal formula. Mike and Marion
were used to this pressure and would wordlessly agree. Jan,
however, was not so tolerant. And the remarks about
Mandy's mode of dress could be the start of one of her
'advice' sessions and Mike, fearing that Jan would one day
tell Mum where to put her advice, had spurred him to head
for the kitchen.

Entering the kitchen Mike had a surprise, Peter the
Sparky.

'Good God, Pete, it's you.'

'Sure is, mate, the one and only.'

He spoke with his strong lilting South Walian accent. Jan

and Mike didn't think that they had a Welsh accent. But on a rare visit to Jan's sister in London, they had been surprised when a bus conductor added a cheerful 'Thanks Taffy,' to his tendering of change.

Mike busied himself filling the kettle. Peter was only about 24 years old but was one of those young men who go bald early and had very little hair. But it suited his head shape and he was, by any standard, good looking, and whenever Mike bumped into him socially or around the town, he had a different good-looking woman in tow. As a self-employed electrician he appeared very successful and always had plenty of work and had even done some work at Mike's lab.

'I saw you with that Barbara bird last night. You want to get there, mate. She's mad for it. Know what I mean?' Pete leered and gave Mike a nudge. 'Yeah, mad for it,' he repeated.

'Yeah, right' Mike replied and quietly closed the kitchen door.

Pete wasn't a quiet sort of bloke.

'Did you take a girlfriend with you, a foursome, was it?' Mike asked tentatively hoping to get some clarification as to what went on and how it worked. What was Roy doing for instance?

'Nah, just me. I try and stick to married women. Safer, innit? Send 'em back to their husbands.'

He grinned again, giving another wink.

'What about Roy, then? Was he there like, um, you know, when you and Barbara were, you know . . . ?'

'Oh, yeah he was there. He did it after me. You want to get there, mate, you're a long time dead, you know, and this is the sixties. Yeah, it was a bloody good night.'

The boiling kettle and Mike's mum interrupted them. Peter busied himself fitting the front of the power point on.

41

'Is that kettle ready, son? How about you, Mr Evans, do you want a cup?'

'No thanks, missus, I've nearly done,' Pete said, struggling to give a non-leering, non-sexual customer smile.

'Yes, it's ready, Mum.'

'Right, see you then, Pete,' Mike said as he headed out of the kitchen and leaving his mother to make and serve the coffee.

'Righto, mate, remember what I told you, get it in.'

As Mike returned to the sitting room, Janice gave him a look that said, 'She's been nagging again'. Mike gave a sympathetic grimace, sat on the big uncomfortable, but fashionable sofa, and lit up a cigarette, offering one to Jan. The coffee was brought in together with orange drinks for the kiddies and general chat ensued. But Mike's mind was elsewhere and busy thinking about Pete's comments.

After a while the children became restless and by general consent it was decided it was time to leave. As they were heading out Mike's mum rather belatedly suggested they could stay for a meal and see his sister.

'No thanks, Mum, we've got friends calling tonight and I've got to get the kids to bed,' Jan said hurriedly, not wishing to stay any longer. Having visitors was news to Mike, but then he realised it was a good ruse to curtail the visit. Although he loved his mother, she could be very demanding and Jan could only take her in small doses. His mother gave a somewhat contemptuous sniff at Jan's refusal and everyone received parting kisses.

'We haven't got anyone calling really, have we?' Mike asked as he pulled out into a gap in the stream of traffic.

'Not until Saturday. Susan and Crow are coming over, but I didn't want to stay any longer. She gets worse, you know. She's now telling me what the kids should wear.'

'Yeah, I know, Jan, but what can we do? It's just how she is.'

They both fell silent but the children continued their excited homeward journey. Many of their trips together were silent now. When they had been courting and driving around in the old van they had sworn exuberantly that they would never get like other couples they passed, sitting side by side with glum down-turned mouths. It seemed, however, they were . . .

The following day, a Saturday, Mike had finished tidying the rubbish in the rear garden and he had cleaned the car, so he thought he deserved some time out. He was proud of the car. It had been an expensive car in its day but was getting on a bit when they bought it. But the previous owners had been the local gas board and it had been chauffeur driven, and was in very good condition, although some of his work mates called it an old-fashioned wreck.

The autumn and winter weather had, so far, been sunny, cold and dry, unlike the summer which had been mostly dull with heavy rain storms, and he had decided to go out for the afternoon to one of their favourite pieces of country-side, complete with a good-size stream and a little waterfall all bordered by tall trees and bushes. The kids loved it, messing about on the water's edge, and in summer they would splash about in the water. On the warmer summer days trout could often be seen jumping out of the water to catch flies and if one stood still and quiet, birds such as moorhens and coot would glide by looking for food amongst the waterweeds. If they were really lucky a heron might be seen strutting about in the shallows, head down catching snack-sized tiddlers. It was a beautiful secluded spot and they had never seen anyone else there. Yet it was only 30 minutes from home. Mike had known the area since he was a kid when he used to cycle out from home, usually on his own, to explore the surrounding countryside or visit his school friend's farm.

Mike used up half a roll of slide film – prints were too

expensive – of the kids mostly, and a couple of landscapes. They had a little picnic and then leisurely walked – except for little Mandy who needed carrying – the mile back to the car, agreeing as they did so what a great time they had had. At times like these in the peaceful rural setting Mike and Jan were relaxed and happy. The natural surroundings and the muted golden and brown autumn colours that still remained softened any outside pressures. It seemed to Mike an immense shame to even think about the human lust for sex in such a place – almost sacrilegious. He feared it might spoil the tranquillity of the place. Yet of course the countryside is where nature, and sex, should be more at home. In fact, he quickly remembered they had spent a lot of time in their courting days in various country locations happily groping and kissing in the back of an old van he owned at the time.

Later that evening, after a home cooked treat of steak and chips they sorted out the children for bed and Mike read them a story, plus a chunk of *John and Janet* for Mandy. He had taught David to read with *John and Janet* books, and was now trying to do the same with Mandy. But it was proving a lot harder. She really wasn't interested and was a fidgety little madam, but lovely with it. Mike and Jan then settled in front of the small black and white television to watch the good old *Morecombe and Wise Show*, always good for a smile if not a laugh. It had been a great day and Mike was feeling content with his lot. He had a good job, a beautiful wife, happy kids, yes, he felt great. But not everything in the garden was rosy. Later that night when they lay spoon-like in bed, Mike gently moved his arm over her breasts and pressed his hardness against her bottom. Janice tugged her nightdress tightly around herself, signalling her rejection of his intentions.

'Sorry, Darl, my period started today.'

'It's OK, love,' Mike murmured, giving her a comforting hug.

At Jan's rejection Mike felt an unpleasant dragging sensation in the depths of his stomach. It was as though all his enthusiasm, his happiness was being pulled out of him. He didn't feel angry, but sad – a sense of loss. After their lovely afternoon out he had wished to share, to consolidate his joy with Jan. After all it was called lovemaking, wasn't it? In fact, the happier he was the more he wanted sex. No, now he was being irrational. For God's sake, Jan couldn't help having a period.

However, Janice had lied.

Janice too was thinking. Not only about her forthcoming role in the musical and the never-ending meal planning and household chores but also about Mike and herself. She felt guilty for refusing him. Yes, she had enjoyed the afternoon. She just didn't want sex. But she asked herself, 'Why couldn't I make the effort?' Jan had hoped her interest and satisfaction from sex with Mike would have improved in marriage but, frankly, she had given up that hope. She believed that for better or worse the pattern of her life was now set. And although her secret sex life satisfied her she still wished she could sate Mike's needs. In fact, she had often wished he could be content with doing what she did. She guessed that he often did satisfy himself and that the girly books he brought from work were part of his sex play. If she had ever asked him she knew he wouldn't be shy in telling her if he did, but of course she hadn't ever said anything for fear of exposing her own activities.

They had, 'though less of late, had long discussions about the situation, which were never resolved. The talks were fairly one-sided with Mike doing most of the talking and all the analysing and questioning, to which she simply couldn't respond. She wished she could be honest and tell him what she thought and felt. But she was no good at formulating philosophical points, and certainly unable to expose what her real thoughts were, nor disclose her personal actions.

Indeed, she vehemently denied ever touching herself. Which Mike had found hard to believe because his reading had taught him women did do it, what exactly he wasn't sure, but whatever it was it was only, as Mike believed, a substitute for 'real' sex with men. Perhaps he was reading the wrong books. However, Mike believed her. He had to because she was the only woman he had known intimately, so he had no others to compare with. And he was beginning to think they had a bigger problem than he had first thought. Why didn't she want to have sex with him as they used to? He was aware that Jan had an exceedingly poor opinion of herself and perhaps it was this that stifled her ability to express any strong opinions, well any opinion at all really. Yet she shouldn't feel that way, she had so many talents, and as Mike often said, repeating what his grandmother used to say, she was 'as clever as bees' knees' to which Jan used to laugh.

Of course, what Mike didn't know was that Janice had read the magazine he had brought from work. Indeed it had fuelled a quick afternoon session of self-pleasuring, the pictures of the naked females reminding her of her own erotic self image she sometimes created in the bedroom mirror, yet at the same time wishing her body looked like those women in the magazine. She also read the letters about wife-swapping on the turned down pages, suspecting Mike had intended her to anyway. She thought it probably did go on somewhere but very unlikely in this town, and couldn't believe Barbara would do that sort of thing. It just seemed too quiet and conventional a place – not glamorous enough for such a revolution. She pondered idly that who would want her anyway, with her supposed fat and stretch-marked stomach. No one would find her attractive. Even so the idea itself was not totally unappealing – in theory.

6

Saturday was a cold wet horrible day, and Mike found it immensely depressing. The house had no central heating and all the windows were dripping with condensation and the deep grey skies matched his mood. Janice had to do some shopping for the evening get together with Crow and Susan so Mike stayed at home with the children whilst Jan went out to do the shopping; it just wasn't worth the stress of dragging them in and out of the shops in the rain.

By late morning the weather had brightened a little and Mike began to return to his more optimistic state. He still had that internal sadness from Jan's rejection the night before, but he wasn't going to let the issue get him down and he looked forward to a drink and a laugh with Crow. However, none one them were regular drinkers and saw no sense in sitting all night in a pub drinking, and they were certainly not sophisticated ones. Mike and Jan, for instance, had, somehow, latched on to cheap sherry from a local off-licence. Take your own bottle and the sherry was drawn from wooden casks, and it only cost seven and sixpence for about a pint and a half. Good stuff. Of course, they all liked spirits but considered them too expensive, unless it was a special occasion.

Whilst Janice was out shopping, Mike spent the morning fitting some new door handles and completing some other small fiddly jobs around the house that he had been putting off for ages. The children were very busy cutting up bits of paper and sticking them everywhere except in their scrap books, but they were happy and their laughter infectious and Mike found himself doing his chores with a smile upon his face.

Janice returned from the shopping trip about lunchtime and quickly knocked up snacks for everyone and then set about preparing 'nibbles' for the evening visitors. Although she said she hated cooking, she always produced something really good. Mike spent the afternoon sorting through some slide photos and at the same time listening to the afternoon play on the radio. He was very fond of the radio, having been brought up with the Home Service, *Children's Hour* and the like. It had just been renamed Radio Four and Mike had been concerned that the content would change. But at the moment it was very much the same, which cheered him greatly.

Evening time was soon upon them, kids put to bed, and bodies bathed and adorned ready for the night's feasting and drinking.

'Yoh, Mike, Jan, how are they hanging, man?'

Crow was in good mood as Jan opened the front door.

'Get in out of the rain and stop messing about,' Jan said with mock severity.

As the tall Crow and the much shorter Susan entered the small sitting room the place seemed to suddenly fill up. The room had one small sofa and two easy chairs, a bookcase and a low table for the portable black and white television. With four people as well it seemed crowded, but on a winter's night such as this, very cosy.

'What you been up to today, Crow?' Mike asked, chewing on a handful of peanuts.

'Not a lot, mate. Work this morning, not like some having a day off, but it was a bit too wet this afternoon to repoint the wall at the back of the house so . . .'

Susan cut him off with 'So he had a go at wallpapering the bedroom. Bloody disaster area now.'

Susan wasn't one to mince her words, and she swore quite a lot, as did Crow. But usually they toned it down a bit when with Mike and Jan, who rarely did and when they did it was comparatively mild, certainly none of the four-letter words. Even at work Mike would only use the naughty words when he considered it expedient not to offend someone who could only communicate by swearing. Although they would have considered themselves 'working class' neither of them had heard quality swearing in the home, so they hadn't ever got into the habit. In fact, it seemed to them the people of their own age that they knew swore a lot, and those with parents from 'the professional classes', swore the most.

'It will take me a week to clean the paste from the floor, mucky sod.'

Crow just grinned at Mike as though to say, bloody women. And he too reached for some peanuts.

'Hey, did you see Morecambe and Wise the other night, and that trick with the paper bag? Bloody good that.'

Mike agreed and they both took another mouthful of peanuts on board.

'Cindy OK, Sue,' Jan asked.

'Yeah, fine, Jan, it's her birthday next week, she'll be two,' replied Susan.

'Time for another one now,' Jan said with enthusiasm. Almost in unison Crow and Susan retorted, 'Not bloody likely.'

'She was an accident. We don't want any more,' Susan added. 'We want to live a bit while we're young.'

'Too right, man, let's have a drink.'

'Good thinking, Crow, I'll get the glasses. We've got two bottles of sherry, you know, like we had before, out of the barrel stuff – or whatever they call it.'

'I think,' Jan said in false cut-glass accent, 'it's called sherry from the wood, darling.'

'Posh bitch,' said Susan laughingly.

'And look what I've brought.'

Crow turned to his jacket which he had deposited indifferently on the floor behind his chair and produced a half bottle of vodka.

'Bloody hell,' said Mike, not used to such largess. 'What's the occasion?'

'I took it out of our Christmas stock. It's only a few weeks away, you know.'

Susan exploded.

'Crow, you bugger, how did you know where I'd hidden it?'

'I peeped,' he said meekly and they all laughed at the silly look on his face.

Jan and Mike were not avid players of music and didn't follow with keen enthusiasm the latest pop record hits. The only reason Mike sometimes watched *Top of the Pops* was to ogle the girls in their miniskirts. So they didn't have a record player, although it was on their mental list of 'household items to get when they could afford it'. The lack of background music didn't bother any of them and they were happy to chat away for hours. Work was usually the first item of conversation for Crow and Mike, and the girls' first discussion point was usually dieting, although television programmes sometimes were dragged in to the conversation.

'Was it busy in work this morning?'

'Nah,' Crow answered, 'pretty quiet really but that Roy bloke got on my tits.'

'Why, what did he do?'

'He's a bossy bastard, only been there five minutes and he thinks he runs the place.'

'He's not so bad, it's just his way.'

50

'Well, he pisses me off, I told him to eff off. If you ask me, he's a bit bloody odd.'

They hadn't started on the vodka but three quarters of a bottle of sherry had already disappeared and they were rapidly becoming comfortably intoxicated. The evening followed a fairly fixed pattern and food, which was eaten at the dining table in the other room, was the halfway break to the drinking.

'Mm, these little pasty things are lovely, Jan, what's in 'em?' Susan sputtered, cramming the food into her mouth.

'Nothing much, dead easy to make. Just potato, corned beef and onions and bits of this and that.'

'We like bits of this and that, don't we, Mike,' Crow interjected in lecherous tone.

'Yeah, we do.' Mike laughed.

'They're off, sex-mad buggers.'

'They're all the same, Sue, no control.'

Mike and Crow ignored the put down and continued stuffing their faces.

'Write this recipe down for me, Jan, I'll have a go at these. You're a great cook.'

The meal over, they settled down to the second half as it were, and sometime during this phase of the evening the subject of sex arose, as it often does in party situations.

The sherry had long gone so the vodka was opened and large drinks were dispensed.

'Hey, Crow, me old mate, has Roy asked you to do a wife swap yet?'

'You what?' he laughed. 'Nah, but he's always going on about it to someone and today he was spouting on about pornography, said it shouldn't be illegal and stuff like that.'

'Well, it's a bit daft really, since that Lady Chatterley thing a couple of years ago. You can read what you want to, but you can't see what you want to. Seems a bit stupid to me. In Sweden and Denmark it's legal and you can buy

51

books and stuff from little kiosks in the street. I mean, now there's the pill women can do what they like.'

Mike spoke with the passion and philosophical zeal of the tipsy.

'Yeah, I suppose you're right. I don't see anything wrong with it either,' conceded Crow as he lit up a fag.

'You wouldn't.' said Susan emphatically.

'For instance.' Mike continued,' if Jan and me took a photo of us doing it, why is that illegal, it's a natural thing isn't it?'

'I've never seen a blue film,' Jan said in a matter-of-fact tone, in an attempt to calm Mike down.

'You haven't missed much,' said Susan, 'seen one seen them all.'

At which, for some reason unknown to the men, Jan and Susan giggled heartily.

'Mind you, the pill is great. Everyone is trying them now. We wouldn't have Cindy if I'd been on it before. He won't use johnnies. Says it doesn't feel the same,' Susan remarked.

'Feels like a Wellington boot on your todger, bloody awful things,' chipped in Crow.

'Mike says the same, that's how we got David. I've just started the pill as well.'

'Here's to the pill' Mike said, raising his glass. 'Best thing since sliced bread.'

They were all well oiled by now and continued talking laughing and drinking enthusiastically.

'Anyway what's all this wife-swapping business, Jan?' Susan said.

'It's all the rage in some places, so they say. Mike had a magazine about it,' Jan replied somewhat disdainfully.

'What's it all about then?' asked Susan with inebriated enthusiasm between gulps of vodka and orange.

'Wish I knew, Sue. I'd like to know how it happens – if you know what I mean,' Mike answered.

'Do you think he's really done it?' What's his wife like, as weird as him I expect?' Crow said disparagingly.

'She seems OK, and Pete, a bloke from the amateur dramatics reckons he done it with her. Mind you, he also reckons he does it twice a night.'

'Seems about right,' Crow agreed with a wry smile. 'Three times on a good night.'

'Oh yeah, ten seconds a week is more like it,' Susan chipped in scornfully.

'Mike fancies her as well,' said Jan, hoping her intervention would distract Mike from saying that they hadn't done it for months.

'I didn't say that,' Mike said defensively.

'You were all over her the other night,' Jan continued.

'That was the booze.'

'Well, I wouldn't mind a swap.' Susan said drunkenly, struggling to stub out her cigarette accurately, her hand waving about before descending heavily into the ashtray.

'Thanks, love,' said Crow with mock hurt.

Susan stood up, with difficulty, and crossed the room towards Mike.

'Yeah, I'll swap with Miky and you go with Jan.'

So saying, she sat down heavily on Mike's lap and began kissing him with abandon. Bloody hell, thought Mike, so this is how it works. Time seemed to have stopped. Someone, somehow, had switched off the light but the gas fire was giving the room a warm red glow. He wished now there was some background music because the room was strangely quiet except for the low hissing of the gas fire and the occasional drone of a passing car. He couldn't see what was happening with Jan and Crow and didn't really care. He was going to see how far this was going to go. He slipped his hand under Susan's jumper and fondled her small breasts through her bra. His other hand started the slow journey under her short skirt and up her thighs towards her knickers. She still didn't stop him and in fact her body felt as thought she had gone to sleep. Soon his fingers were around the edge of her knickers touching hair and soft warm skin. Christ, this is great he thought, kissing her neck again as he tried to open her legs a little wider.

'Oh God, I feel sick,' moaned Susan.

7

The alarm clock was screaming, seven o'clock, seven o'clock. Time to get up. Sunday morning, and Mike had to be in work by eight. Mike's head was not in a good condition, it felt extremely heavy and it was an enormous effort to lift it from the pillow. But lift it he must. He struggled out of the bed, the bedclothes contriving to pull him back in. He was not feeling too lively.

Downstairs he made coffee and sat alone, drinking and smoking, the hot smoke hitting his raw lungs. The coffee began its work soothing his throat and waking his brain. What a night, all that booze – and Susan. Janice and he hadn't spoken, as yet, about the evening's events. Sorting out Susan and getting her in the taxi, Crow didn't have a car, had taken some time and it had gone midnight, late for a working day, which it was for Mike and Crow, before they had fallen into bed utterly exhausted and drunk.

Mike forced some breakfast cereal into his body and set off to the factory. His eyes ached with effort of driving and he was glad it was only a short distance.

'Oh God, my head,' whined Crow, as with shaky hands he tried accurately to pour the solvent into the resin sample.

'Christ, I'm not much better,' Mike said sympathetically. 'How's Sue this morning?'

'Alive, I think. She was really out of it last night,' replied

Crow and they both gave a somewhat feeble and embarrassed laugh.

'Look at it this way Crow, it can only get better. By two o'clock we'll be OK.'

'Man, I hope you're right,' said Crow disbelievingly.

Bob approached with his usual sardonic grin on his face.

'Heavy night, boys?'

'You could say that,' Crow retorted coldly – he seemed to be developing a hate complex against Roy.

'I've bought that camera I was on about the other night, Mike. When do you think you can call and have a look at it?'

'Don't know at the minute, Roy. Can I let you know?'

'Yep, fine, don't leave it too long, though. I want to get cracking with it – if you know what I mean,' he said leering with his very best leer.

During the morning shift Crow didn't mention any intimate details of the previous night. Perhaps from his point of view there weren't any. Or, of course, he just didn't care either way. In fact, Mike found it interesting how extraordinary experiences and occurrences can so very quickly fade into ordinariness. The memory may remain but the strangeness of the original experience is somehow absorbed. Mike, however, had been, and still was, massively stimulated by the experience. If that was wife swapping then he was all for it. He was still somewhat stunned by how quickly it had all happened, good old Sue. It had been a long time since he had touched a woman in that way and the excitement of the unfamiliar had reminded him of his early days with Jan. Not that Susan would be his first choice as a swapping partner. She was a little bit too brash for Mike's tastes and her mouth and smile were not particularly to his liking and he would have to like the personality. He couldn't go with just any woman. But he wouldn't actually refuse, not in the current sexless marital situation. And as Pete had reminded him, 'You're a long time dead'. But Mike really didn't have that sort of confidence with women, but instead of backing away is why, in 'safe' situations, he did all that flirting, such as at the am dram the other night.

'Is it break time yet? I've got to have a coffee and a fag, I'm gasping,' Crow said, interrupting Mike's thoughts.

Mike was back home and eating Sunday roast by 2.30 p.m. The meal over, the children returned to their play and Jan and Mike remained seated at the dining table, smoking and drinking coffee. Outsiders looking in at the pair might be forgiven for thinking that they were looking at strangers in a café. The room itself added to the illusion. The walls were papered in popular wood chip and magnolia emulsion paint. It was sparsely furnished, with the dining table and chairs, another smaller table, which the children used for their play, a small two-seater sofa and on a shelf beside the gas fire, a small tropical aquarium, one of Mike's interests. Basically, it was the room used by the kids for play, their upstairs rooms being, for most of the year, too cold to play in. Jan and Mike were still not at their best. Both were tired from the previous night's revelry.

Jan was first to speak.

'Did Crow say anything in work today?'

'About last night you mean? No nothing. You know Crow, nothing seems to bother him.'

'You were enjoying yourself with Susan,' she said quietly.

'Didn't you, with Crow?'

'No, and I didn't want to do anything and I don't think he fancied me. I think he thought that I'm fat. Sue is skinny.'

Mike was not in the mood for deep discussion, or recriminations.

'You're not fat and she isn't that skinny, and you couldn't have done anything anyway, if it had gone that far. You said you were having a period. And you didn't want sex, you haven't for months.'

'You started it anyway,' Jan said defensively, ignoring his comments.

'Started what?'

'You went on about wife swapping, I didn't want any such thing.'

'Look, Jan, what are you saying? What happened last night was my fault? If anyone started it, it was Sue.'

'She was drunk.'

'We were all drunk, for Christ's sake, but it was bloody good fun and I enjoyed it. Right? And if I get the chance I'll do it again – all the way.'

He stubbed his cigarette in the ashtray and went into the sitting room, pushing their black cat, named with original inspiration by the kids, Blackie, off his chair and switched on the radio.

Jan was still at the dining table; tears were welling in her eyes. She wanted to tell him she was sorry for not being the wife he wanted, for lying about her period the other night, but she couldn't.

'Mum, aren't you and Daddy friends now?' chirped David.

Jan burst into tears.

Mike sat alone listening to the radio and regretting the row. He hated seeing Jan upset and he was a little tearful himself. He hated rows and once again he had that unpleasant hollow, dead feeling in his stomach, that sense of loss. But what have I done? She obviously doesn't feel the same about me any more. I go to work and I work on the house. God, it's not as though I went out behind her back, she was there and nothing really happened. I've never been with another woman, not all the way, and even that was before I met Jan.

His experience with Susan had showed him what he was missing, the thrill and the excitement. He well remembered his feelings after the first time Jan and he had made love, that strangely egoistic exaltation he experienced from Jan's virginity, not for the virginity itself but for the fact that she hadn't trusted or liked anyone else enough to be the first.

Jan looked sexy, had a voluptuous body, and big blue come-to-bed eyes and yet wasn't interested in sex. He couldn't understand it. He longed to share and experience her sexuality, her passion. He wanted them to be happy, to create happy memories together. In fact, he considered it his responsibility, his duty, to care for Jan and the children. As for the sex, it was natural, fun, and it was cheap entertainment – he smiled at that amusing idea. But seemingly Jan had lost what interest she had in all that. But he hadn't. Now he wanted to experience other women, he wanted pleasure, he wanted sex.

But these thoughts now led Mike to another emotion. He was feeling guilt, guilty of thinking what he was thinking. It wasn't the direction he thought he would ever contemplate. He had always desired and worked for perfection in their marriage and believed that Jan had wanted the same. They had had an intense but conventional courtship and engagement and a March wedding, for the income tax rebate, and wrote love letters to each other even though they met virtually every day. Mike, with his energetic inventiveness, would sometimes write extra messages of love in invisible ink between the normal lines, which needed heat to make readable. However, Mike's clues as to the necessity of applying heat were so obscure, such as 'This letter needs the warmth of your heart', that Jan never got to read them. But it was fun. Yes, everything used to be OK. It now appeared that all this was in danger. However, and it was a big however, he definitely didn't want to leave Jan and the kids, nor Jan to leave him. As long as they stayed together there was hope that things would improve.

What a puzzling business it was, being a human being.

The remaining five morning shifts passed uneventfully,

and Mike and Janice, with a wordless hug and impassionate kiss, had returned to normal. Well, what had become normal for them that is, a sort of stand-off. It's sad how very fragile our relationships with others are and how quickly friends, wives, and husbands can drift apart and, in some cases, became total enemies, sometimes to go as far as contemplating murder. Little wonder that in the outside world, countries can so easily turn to war.

Mike had arranged to call on Roy on the evening of the last shift, a Friday, this Friday.

'That was really good.'

Home-cooked fresh fish and chips were one of his favourites, to be honest most foods were. He had a big appetite.

'Good. It was nice, even though I say so myself,' Jan said with a self-satisfied smile.

'Can I go and watch the telly, Mum?'

'Of course, love.'

'And me, Mummy,' piped Mandy.

'Off you go then. Pass the lighter, please,' Jan asked Mike, as she picked up the packet of cigarettes lying on the table.

Mike pushed the lighter towards her.

'What time are you going to that Roy's place?'

She emphasised 'that,' and lit up her cigarette.

'I said about half past seven. Are you sure you don't want to come with me?'

'No, you go. It's too late to get a babysitter anyway. You will be a good boy, won't you? And if you can't be good, be careful,' Jan added with a smile.

Christ, Mike was astounded at Jan's good humour. Did she mean that he could indulge in any sexual adventure that might occur at Roy's? No. He couldn't believe that.

'You don't mind me going do you? It's only to see his camera.'

'Now that's a new line.' She was smiling again. 'Anyway,

Mum and Dad might be calling after their Bingo session and I've got to start learning my part for the show.'

Mike wondered what the hell was going on. Jan was in such a good mood he thought it might be better to stay at home. But that was being too optimistic.

'I don't have to go tonight but we've got Christmas shopping to do tomorrow and we'll be late back from town and . . .'

Jan cut him off mid flow.

'You go. It's OK, I really don't mind, you go and enjoy yourself.'

Now he really was surprised.

As Mike drove towards the western end of town heading for Roy's flat, there was some time for reflection. He was happy because Jan was happy. He pondered why this should be, perhaps it was the Christmas spirit, it was about four weeks away and Jan liked getting ready for Christmas even though it meant a lot of work and preparation. He also enjoyed the time, although he didn't have to do very much towards it. He also began to speculate what was ahead of him at Roy's place. Mike had washed and preened as one does when anticipating new intimate encounters, taking extra care with those special little corners. His careful preparations had sparked off memories of his courting days with Jan, memories which he pushed to the back of his mind, not wishing to contaminate them with what he might be involved with at Roy's.

Even though he wasn't certain anything would happen, he was hoping something would. In a way he was strangely nervous, the nervousness of the unknown, rather like a job interview, and he had a couple of butterflies arguing in his stomach. And he smiled to himself at the image of Roy and Barbara interviewing him as to his suitability for a wife swap. Deep inside he wasn't a very confident person but his ego wouldn't allow him to give in to this weakness. It had often crossed his mind that he would like to be like the men who could have sex with women they didn't know, prostitutes or other total strangers. And what about the blokes in those blue films at work, how could they perform in front of the cameras? But there again he mused; did they have confidence or were they simply indifferent? Wasn't it almost worthy to overcome a lack of confidence or fear, rather than be indifferent or not have the fear in the first place?

'Mike, come in, you found the place all right?'

Roy greeted him with enthusiasm.

'Yeah, couldn't miss it really.'

'We're on the top floor come on up. Jan not with you?'

'No she's studying her lines for that musical thingy – big place, Roy,' Mike said looking around him.

The stairs weren't exactly grand but at least twice the width of his stairs at home. Classy-looking old paintings hung on the walls and real flock wallpaper. As they approached the landing he was also struck by the size of the doors to the rooms, which opened onto the corridor, and by the ornate old brass doorknobs. 'How the other half live,' he muttered to himself.

'We don't notice it,' Roy replied nonchalantly.

'Here we are, go on in, Mike.'

He pushed open a door and followed Mike in.

The room faced the old harbour and had views across the municipal gardens to the popular sandy bay, now lit by moonlight but in daylight it must be a fantastic vista.

The room was large, and bigger than Mike's sitting room and 'dining' room put together, and to Mike's mind sumptuous. There was even a grand piano, for Christ's sake. He was, to say the least, a little overawed and felt uncomfortable, a bit out of place. Apart from Liberace's piano, there was ample space for two large sofas and in front of each, a low table. Against one wall stood a long side table adorned with various pieces of china and silver and other nick-nacks were placed around the room. The opposite wall had a large open fire, the hearth of which was taken up by an old-fashioned electric fire, much embellished with gilt mouldings. The fire wasn't on but the room was pleasantly warmed by the central heating – what luxury he thought. The lighting was a mixture of ceiling lights, standard lamps and wall lights, and, not a piece of woodchip wallpaper in sight.

'Nice place,' Mike said rather inadequately.

'Not bad, is it? It's not really ours. Belongs to Bab's parents.'

'Oh, right,' Mike mumbled, adding, 'Where's this wonder camera then?'

'I'll get it in a minute. Sit down, have a ciggy.'

Bob offered him a cigarette and he was grateful for it, something normal to do in the unusual surroundings. Roy pushed a huge glass ashtray towards him. 'Another priceless antique probably,' Mike thought ungraciously.

In his own surroundings Roy's manner seemed a little less nervous, more relaxed, but his eyes, or what could be seen of them behind the lenses, still flickered uneasily.

As they sat smoking and nattering about this and that, Mike was wondering where Barbara was. Then, as though his thinking had summoned her, she entered the room.

Stubbing out his fag, Roy got up.

'I'll go and get the camera I think I left in the bedroom.'

He gave Mike a lecherous grin.

'Hiya,' Barbara murmured as she beside him on the sofa. She was stark naked.

Jan was sitting in the small front sitting room drinking coffee and smoking as she went over her lines for her part in the Baray Arts musical show. There weren't many spoken bits as it was mostly a singing role, but she liked to get it right, to make a good job of it. Her parents had visited and left, and it was now about 10.30 p.m. and she began to wonder where Mike was, and what he was doing. The thought of him being with Barbara or, come to that, any woman, had initially disturbed her. She felt a mixture of jealousy, anger and inadequacy, and yet, perversely, she was experiencing a sense of excitement and relief. Excitement from imagining what they might be doing, perhaps something thrilling and new that she herself would like to be adventurous enough to try, and she also had a degree of elation from the possibility of relief from Mike's sexual demands upon her. But at what cost? Would he fall in love with someone else? Would he leave her? She also wondered if Barbara enjoyed it more than she did. Was she better at it? She concluded she must be if she went in for that sort of behaviour. Most of the feelings of anger were directed at the 'creepy bloke Roy' for starting it all in the first place. It would be nice if everything just stayed still, without change, as they used to be. Of course, much anger was aimed at Mike himself for even considering getting involved. Wasn't she a good mother? She looked after the house and kids, made clothes for them. She did her best. Everything used to be OK and again she blamed 'that' Roy for the whole business. However, she didn't actually feel threatened by Barbara as she thought she was bit dozy, a bit of a scatter-brain and really wasn't Mike's type. But, of course, there were always other women.

Deep down Jan was positive that Mike wouldn't leave her and the kids. He wasn't the sort of person to throw anything away. He was a hoarder of material and sentimental objects and in fact still kept a box of his childhood toys. She believed that this trait applied to relationships too. He always stuck by people, as indeed did Jan, and since she had known him it had been rare for him to cast anyone aside, even if he found them a pain in the backside. It was a risk but she really didn't think that anything would come of it

64

and creepy Roy was all talk. And she hoped by letting him go without a fuss he would get the swapping nonsense out of his system. She felt comforted by these thoughts and momentarily allowed herself a naughty idea – that she might like to watch people having sex – might like to watch Mike with another woman.

Roy gave a final gasp of release and, like a buck rabbit, collapsed sideways from off Barbara's body. Barbara slowly rose from the bed, pushing her dishevelled hair from her pink-flushed face and Mike laid the camera down on the bedside table.

8

'No, no, no not like that, you should come on from the left – the left.'

Bill, the am dram supremo immaculately dressed as usual in slacks and shirt, complete with neat cravat, shook his head in utter frustration. The poor girl he had shouted at looked as though she was about to explode into tears, and Bill quickly regained his normally calm composure and stepped forward onto the stage.

'Look, luv, I'm sorry I shouted. Everything's fine. Just try it one more time. OK?'

Turning and coming back down off the stage he raised his eyes skyward and gave Mike a grin that said, 'God, why do I do this?' Mike had returned the smile, together with a sympathetic nod.

It was Saturday afternoon and Mike had taken the kids to the local park after dropping Jan at the community hall for rehearsals. They had planned to go Christmas shopping that morning but had decided to wait until they could do it without the children in tow. They would have their day in town seeing Father Christmas in his grotto nearer to the great day but meanwhile the kiddies would have a day at Grandma's whilst Mike and Jan did the bulk of the present buying in relative peace. By 3.30 p.m. it had begun to get dark so they had left the park and returned to the hall to collect Janice from her acting labours and head off home for tea.

'Is Jan ready to come home, Bill?'

'Give us a half hour or so, Mike. All right?'

'Yeah, sure, you're the boss,' Mike said, laughing.

'Don't remind me. No, luv, the left, the left side,' and off he went.

The children were happily munching sweets as they explored the dusty corners of the old community building and Mike lit up a cigarette and sat watching the antics on stage. In the comparative tranquillity of the darkened auditorium area Mike, for the millionth time, relived the extraordinary moments of the previous evening at Roy's palatial flat. If someone had asked him then how he felt afterwards he would have found it difficult to describe the mixture of emotions. Yes, it had been an exceedingly erotic episode, like something out of the readers' letters in the girly magazines, in which people described their fantastic sexual adventures, either real or imagined, in great detail. But his adventure had been all too real, and fantastic. Yet here he was, with the kids, doing his very ordinary waiting-for-Jan game. He found it so odd, and struggled to get to grips with the enormous contrast of yesterday evening.

In some ways it had been very funny. Coping with the new Polaroid camera had not been easy. After taking each photo the film then had to be placed in a thin metal holder and placed, as the maker recommended, under the armpit for the warmth to develop the image, a very uncomfortable and tedious task, epecially when naked, and aroused, and particularly as the image sometimes was too light or dark and the whole business had to be repeated after adjustments to the camera. Mike just wanted, to put it crudely, 'get it in' and get on with the real business. He had been a bit concerned that he wouldn't be able to perform satisfactorily in the unusual situation and it had been a couple of months since he had 'real' sex. But he need not have worried. All had worked very well. However, Roy was insistent that perfect photos were obtained, and of as many positions as possible, and seemed more interested in this aspect than in the sex itself. In fact, he made it tacitly clear it was his show and he was in charge. Later, however, it was Mike's turn, as it were, with Babs, and Roy was far from his mind.

It had been a very interesting evening, which had progressed effortlessly, and in a matter-of-fact manner, and to Mike's surprise without alcohol, as though such happenings were a daily occurrence. Perhaps for Roy and Babs they were. One of the interesting facets of the evening for Mike had been seeing, in the flesh, another man's erection. In Roy's case a circumcised one. And he wondered if Roy had been equally interested in his uncircumcised one. Afterwards, fully clothed and sitting and drinking coffee and chatting, mostly to Roy, about nothing at all, seemed particularly odd. In any event, it was an experience he would like to repeat, although without Roy, and the camera.

After Mike had left the flat and was alone in the car he initially experienced elation from the exciting sexual adventure itself, and from the fact that he was involved in something new and sophisticated. Well, sophisticated in Mike's eyes. After all, it wasn't everyone who behaved as he had and this thought gave him a confidence of a sort he hadn't previously had. He also found it fascinating to realise that no one could tell by appearance he had done anything so out of the ordinary. It was in a way the 'I have a secret' syndrome and when in an optimistic mood he had a vision of himself and Jan as a really swish couple, which was, in their sexless marriage, a very erroneous view. And perversely, when he thought of Janice sitting at home he felt a little sickened in his gut with guilt and the all too familiar sense of emptiness. Yet at the same time he felt a strange sense of pride, and yes, love towards Jan because seemingly she had allowed him this freedom. In many ways the whole business was more of an ego-trip than an erotic exploration and his orgasm the aim of the game. His guilt wasn't really about the sex, but all the other, now broken, values he believed were inherent in the commitment to marriage. Perhaps he was basically old fashioned. It might be nice if Jan would share this new world then, possibly, this dichotomy of emotions would disappear, but that hardly seemed likely.

Suddenly cool soft hands were over his eyes.

'Guess who?' spoke a female voice he didn't readily recognise.

'Diana Dors,' said Mike with false inspiration.

'Nearly right, Julie Thomas,' the voice said with a laugh as the hands were removed.

Mike turned to see a ginger-haired blue-eyed girl about his own age. They both laughed at the silliness of their comments. Diana Dors, the film star, was a blonde, Julie had long ginger hair and lacked the hourglass figure but she was attractive, had an acceptable smile, and he liked women with long hair.

'Well, hello, Julie, I'm Mike,' he said in what he thought was a very suave tone.

'I know, Roy told me.'

'Roy, is he here?'

'No not today. He's not in this bit of the show. I'm a friend of Babs. And I know your Jan, of course.'

'Oh right, I see, Are you in this show?'

'Only the chorus.'

'So you're a chorus girl.'

'Mm, and you know what they are like don't you?' she murmured seductively.

'Do I?' said Mike, again in his best suave tone.

'Some can be very naughty girls – well so I've heard.' Then, changing the subject, she added, 'Why don't you have a go – at the singing?'

'God, me? I can't sing a note, anyway I'm chief babysitter.'

'We haven't got any kids so no problem there. Listen, why don't you and Jan come over one night to our place? I'll ring you shall I? What's your number?'

'Um, we're not on the phone.'

Mike felt a pang of inferiority at the lack of a phone – again.

'That's OK, I'll see Jan then, shall I?'

'Yeah, fine.'

'OK bye, got to go.'

Giving him a wide smile and a little squeeze of his arm, she hurried off behind the stage.

Mike sat staring after her totally bemused.

'Whew what was all that about? Bloody hell, she was flirting with me, giving me the come on. That's a first for me for sure. Ginger hair, that's different, long too, mm very nice. But why me? Women just don't do that to me. What the hell is going on?'

Then inspiration struck. Roy, it was something to do with him. Or Babs, of course. Had he joined some sort of underground sex club? The occurrence also seemed to confirm his idea the am dram was full of people on the look out for a bit of the other. Mike suddenly had a stab of concern. He really didn't want the world knowing what he and Jan were doing or not doing. What if it got back to his other friends or, god forbid, his mother – or Jan's parents? Rationality rapidly returned as he considered that possibility to be highly unlikely.

'Dad, can we go now? I'm bored,' David moaned.

'And me, Daddy,' added Mandy.

'Mum won't be long now, sweetheart, then we can go home.'

As he spoke Jan came out of a side door that led to the stage.

'Mummy,' the children said in unison as they ran to her and clasped her around the legs.

'There's a lovely welcome. Hi, Mike, everything all right?' Jan said brightly, smiling happily at the children's loving reception. 'Why has she got those clothes on?' Jan said, looking at Mandy's attire and realising they weren't the same outfit she had started out with.

'Ah, well, she did her usual trick of getting in the water. Good job we carry spares.'

Mandy loved water and would take her clothes off and jump in any large puddle, garden pond or lake, at any time of year. On this day she hadn't even bothered to take her clothes off and was into the shallows of the lake before Mike could stop her. It was a worrying habit and meant she had to be closely watched when near water.

'Oh, it doesn't matter, as long as you had a good time.'

'Yep, we've been on the swings in the park, and we fed the swans on the lake until it got too dark. Didn't we, kids? Ready to go now?'

'Yes. Come on, you ratbags, home we go,' Jan said swinging Mandy up into her arms.'

'What's a ratbag, Mum?' said David thoughtfully.

Outside the weather had taken a turn for the worse and a thick fog shortened their view of the world.

'Bloody hell, I hate driving in fog. It was clear when we got here. What a change,' moaned Mike.

In truth, in a well-lit town fog made very little difference to the art of driving. In dark country lanes it could be a different matter.

And in a more cheerful tone he added, 'Here's the car. All aboard the good ship Austin.'

'It's not a ship really, Dad', piped David, his early development of a sense of logic killing Mike's attempt at a child-level joke.

And Mike thought that those *John and Janet* books with which he had taught David to read had a lot to answer for.

'Well, let's just pretend it is. Raise anchor – off we go.'

'You are funny, Dad,' said David with a laugh.

Doors were closed, children settled, and the car pulled away to make the 20 minute drive home.

'How did the rehearsals go? Bill was struggling with one girl. Kept coming on from the wrong side or something.'

'That was Meryl, works in Barclays bank.'

'Blimey, wouldn't like to have an account there,' Mike joked.

'Hey, do you know someone called Julie?'

'Julie Thomas? Yes, her husband comes into the hotel bar quite a lot. Nice sort of chap, quite good looking,' Jan, added thoughtfully.

'Well, she said she's going to ask you if we want to go over to their place. For a meal I suppose.'

Mike remained silent on the other possible nuances of the invitation.

'Um yeah, OK,' Janice murmured thoughtfully

Mike concentrated on the driving and apart from the kids chattering in the rear seat the atmosphere fell silent. Jan, however, was recalling her barmaid chats with Julie's husband, Tony, during her lunchtime bar work at the Baray Hotel, a large hotel that had seen better days, although it was fighting to regain its place in the town. Situated in the more affluent western side of the town, its lunchtime patrons were mainly the retired middle class, shopkeepers and the like, and, surprisingly, off-duty police, presumably because the chances of meeting any of their criminal 'clients' in such a place were minimised. Certainly the place wasn't frequented by the local prosies, prostitutes, as were the pubs nearer the dockland's area. Tony was, so he said, with a playful bar room sense of mystery, 'something in the council offices'. For all Jan knew he could be the cleaner, or the Director of Finance.

In the few months Janice had been in the job she had realised that men say things to barmaids, which they wouldn't normally say. And it's a fact that people tend to treat certain workers, like bar staff and the back of a taxi driver's head, as anonymous listeners, when, of course, they are not. The opportunity for blackmail could be enormous.

Tony appeared at first glance to be just like such men, full of nonsense. But Jan liked him, even found him attractive, partly because he had nice hands – this was Janice's thing. The hands had to be right, she didn't want any sort of hand touching her body. Mike had nice hands, strong but gentle and somehow, sexy. She had the idea that in many ways hands could express the nature of the person. Certainly whenever she did some sketching, she found hands very difficult to draw. Anyway, even when she told him that she knew his wife he still talked to Janice in the same way. He was a joky sort of chap, dark-haired, brown-eyed and of middling height and a bit overweight. She felt quite safe with his suggestive remarks and innuendo. After all, she had the bar counter as a physical barrier, and indeed her own blossoming barmaid patter and growing self-confidence as a second line of defence – should it be needed. And just as the men flirted with her in the safe environment of the hotel, she could do the same and walk away at the end of her stint just as the men did.

Expanding her thoughts further, Jan knew that she would want to be in control of any encounter such as Mike might have had at Roy's. Not that anything explicit had been said about his evening there, and at the same time, she did, and didn't want to know.

But knowing Mike's appetite as she did, she was pretty certain that he had sex with Babs. She also sensed he would like it if she would 'experiment' as well, preferably at the same time and place. Well, she might, but under her own terms in her own time. Perhaps she would find out if it were hers or Mike's fault that had lead to dissatisfying sex. Perhaps she could find enjoyment from the flirting and the controlling factor alone. After all, any man she might go with wouldn't be her husband and she could walk away from the situation at any time.

'We ought to get a telephone put in, what do you think?' said Mike, breaking into Jan's thoughts.

'A phone? What made you think of getting a phone?' Jan carried on talking not waiting for a explanation, for which Mike was grateful. 'Yeah, I suppose it would be handy. Cost a bit though and you have to wait for ages, and then it's only a party line we'll have to share. But I'll ask my mum what they paid for theirs. But I think we should leave it until after Christmas. I've really got to get on with the shopping. I've done hardly anything.'

'OK, and don't worry so much, you say that every year. Here we are kiddie winks – home sweet home.'

'What does home sweet home mean, Dad?' David enquired.

But Mike's day of surprises were not over. Once in the house the children dashed to their play table in the dining room and Jan headed for the kitchen and busied herself with getting a meal ready. Mike was putting the camera he had taken with him back into the cupboard under the stairs when suddenly Mandy gave an urgent shout.

'Daddy, Daddy, the fishies are all funny.'

'Funny, what do mean sweetheart?'

Mike's tone was one of quiet amusement, rather than of concern, but on entering the dining room he saw to his utter surprise that the fish were dead. All of them. Their lifeless bodies slowly drifting this way and that.

Mike spent the next day cleaning out the fish tank and

disposing of the previous inhabitants. It was a dismal task and he was glad when it was over. What exactly went wrong he wasn't sure but he suspected the thermostat was faulty. Although it was only a few years old he decided to buy a new one when he set the tank up again, if he bothered at all. For he now had an exciting new hobby to pursue because he intended to call on Babs when he knew Roy wouldn't be there, just to see what would happen. Lots, he hoped. Then there was Julie. How was that going to develop?

Janice and the children had been very sympathetic about the disaster and Mandy had even offered him some of her sweets as consolation. To everyone's surprise they missed the colourful mute creatures, and the empty unlit tank now looked like a black hole on the shelf.

The incident had temporarily dampened his euphoric mood brought about by his recent satisfying experience, but with a Sunday roast under his belt, he was soon back to his normal self. Sitting comfortably by the gas fire, the cat curled up on his lap, he was reading a book on hypnosis he'd borrowed from the town library. He liked the library, the hushed quietness of the place, the smell of the books mixed with the polish used on the shiny wooden block floor. He went quite often and would pick up any title that took his fancy. It might be a book on gardening, psychology or a science-fiction novel. But the book on hypnosis was a bit of a disappointment, a bit clinical, and mostly contained cases of mental disturbances that had been analysed using hypnosis. It was also rather old, having been printed in the 1940s. What Mike wanted to know was how to hypnotise, just out of curiosity. However, there were some consolations because some of the cases were about problems that had a sexual background and he found them quite, arousing.

It was about 7.00 p.m. when there was a rapping at the front door.

'Someone at the door, Mike,' shouted Janice from upstairs where she was getting the children to bed.

'Yes, OK, OK, I bet it's those bloomin' kids again wanting to sing us carols. If they start any earlier it will be in August.'

Both Mike, and the cat, were displeased at the disturbance and Mike headed for the door with irritable haste. As he opened the door his scowling face did a rapid double take and broke into a smile of surprise.

'Julie?'

His voice had a questioning tone. 'Come in, come in, it's blowing a gale out there.'

As she stepped hurriedly into the hallway, she returned his smile and gave his arm a little squeeze of familiarity, her forget-me-not blue eyes briefly gazing into his.

'Can't stop, Mike. Is Jan in?'

'Yes, she's seeing to the kids.'

As he spoke Jan came down the stairs.

'Hi, Jules, come in sit down a minute.'

'Can't stop, Jan, I'm just going home. I've been to rehearsals all afternoon and I thought I'd kill two birds . . .'

She didn't finish the saying but rushed on breathlessly.

'Bill wants to know can you come to rehearsals tomorrow evening and can you and Mike come over to our place next Saturday?'

Jan, much to Mike's surprise, responded almost as quickly and breathlessly as Julie's delivery.

'Yes, lovely, that's great. What time do you want us?'

'About seven if that's OK, Jan. Not too early with the kids to see to is it?'

'No, that's fine, thanks, Jules.'

'Great. See you then. You know where we are, don't you?'

'Yeah, number forty-two, right?'

'Yes, OK then, see you both then. Bye, both. Must dash. Bye.'

She rushed out and they heard her crashing gears in the little Ford Anglia and speeding away despite the fog.

'Bloody hell, talk about a whirlwind,' Mike said, letting out a relaxing sigh.

The house seemed quiet, hushed somehow now that she had gone.

'She's always in a rush. I don't know how she would cope if she had kids,' Jan retorted, climbing the stairs once again to check on the children.

Mike returned to his book but his mind had been energised by the inrush of possibilities that Julie's invitation had engendered and his reading was now boring.

'Things are looking up and up. Sue, Babs and now Julie, and she certainly didn't waste any time making the invitation. It was only yesterday that I spoke to her.'

Mike felt pleased with himself. He was still hungry for sex: perhaps ravenous would be more accurate. He still desired Janice and obviously his frustration in this area simply added to his appetite He had a lot of catching up to do.

He smiled a self-satisfied smile. In a very short time he had changed. His ideas, his beliefs, had modified, almost on a daily basis, and he was now beginning to look upon women as pure pleasure machines. The very fact of how their bodies worked, with their virtually invisible excitable bits and their lunar cycles, were an enigmatic marvel. The differing body shapes, even their bewildering variety of underwear and fascinating pieces of elastic and silk, all interested him greatly.

All around him there were magazines, books and newspaper articles extolling 'free' sex and the 'swinging sixties'. But he hadn't ever been a follower of fashion or passing crazes. Mike just wasn't interested and he tried to stay neutral. In fact, Jan always had to work hard to persuade him to make the most modest changes in dress. But, of course, there is always an exception to the rule and this particular social change he was caught up in, seemed to be just his cup of tea, and the women he was meeting seemed to have the same attitude to sex that he had. They actually wanted it. It hadn't crossed his mind that perhaps it was for reasons other than for simple sexual pleasure that they did what they did. His dislike of parties had also diminished. With the possibility of sensual excitement that was present at these gatherings he found them far more tolerable now that they had a purpose.

However, all Mike's self-satisfied reflections were cruelly halted by the sudden realisation he was working afternoon shifts that week and on that date. He would have to make some arrangements at work, because he had no intention of missing the party.

Later with kiddies in bed, Mike and Jan settled in front of the television, with, at least on the surface, a reasonable degree of domestic contentment. She with her script, he with his book.

At the other side of town, however, there was greater activity.

Roy was sitting in his elegant lounge looking at photographs, some taken the night of Mike's visit, and some others of Babs that he had taken since. He was laying them out in rows on one of the large coffee tables and occasionally he would study a print more closely before adding it to the others on the table. He was intent, serious, unsmiling and tense. At intervals he paused and took a drink from a small glass bottle of Coka Cola before returning to his task. Barbara, looking harassed and dishevelled, entered the room and began picking up scattered toys and placing them into a large cardboard toy box. Roy raised his head from his perusals.

'Get your clothes off.'

'Not now, please, I really don't want to, Roy, I'm tired. I've just put the girls to bed.'

'Do as you're bloody well told. Unless you want me to persuade you.'

He spoke in his quiet, tremulous and yet, menacing tone.

'Oh God, I really don't want to, please,' Babs pleaded in equally quiet manner, almost under her breath in case the loudness of her protests would anger him further.

'Get your clothes off now.'

She slowly and reluctantly began removing her clothes.

'Don't take all bloody day about it, bitch. Sit there opposite me.'

She didn't really need telling where to sit and she knew what he wanted. She finished undressing and sat in the large upholstered chair facing Roy, who sat still, fully clothed.

'Open your legs wider. Show it to me. Stick your fingers in. Go on, tell me what you're doing. Go on do it. Tell me what Mike did to you. Tell me, go on. Did he put his fingers in. Did he? Tell me.'

His voice now had a harsher, urgent edge, his face taking on a pink-flushed hue. His small brown eyes behind the lens of his glasses were shining lustfully. He had unzipped his trousers and he was fondling his growing hardness while Barbara related the events of the previous Friday evening with vulgar exaggeration.

'Dirtier, say it dirtier. Go on, do it.'

He suddenly drained the Cola bottle, crossed the short distance to Babs, and delivered a stinging slap to her face, dropping the empty bottle onto her lap and returning to his seat.

'Put it in. Do it now, useless bitch. Put it in deep, push it in and out. Go on, harder, faster. Squeeze your tits. Do it, and pull the nipples hard. Tell me what you're doing and what Mike and Pete did to you. Do it, for Christ's sake. I want to come now,' he snarled.

In the affluent surroundings, the tableaux created by the two people was harsh and incongruous, and Babs, with sad eyes, and in her lonely chair, obeyed.

9

Monday afternoon came all too soon, and a dark dull one at that. The forecast had predicted snow, but it was work for Mike, and Janice at the hotel, and he drove off with his usual lack of enthusiasm. However, rather like his previous reluctance for parties, he knew that when he got there and the shift banter began he would feel more cheerful. Crow could usually be relied upon to raise a smile or two with his carefree manner and his witty remarks. He could be a real tonic. Mike was a few minutes late arriving, and in the lab Crow was already at work and Mike changed quickly and joined him at the lab bench.

'Hi, man. Have you heard the latest rumour?'

Crow spoke quietly so as not to cause his hands to shake as he carefully poured the contents of a measuring cylinder into a test tube.

'What rumours are these then?' Mike replied, smiling and expecting yet another of Crow's amusing quips.

'No, really, man, we're going to be taken over, whatever that means.'

'Taken over?'

Mike stopped what he was doing and looked at Crow.

'Yep. One of the big oil companies, buying the whole site. The plant the lab, everything.'

'Bloody hell. Is that good news or bad? And where did you get all this from?'

'John, on the morning shift. Some bloke came and told them the news. They reckon we're going to get a pay rise and help with a mortgage, if you've got one. Which you and me have. So it's good news.'

'Well, it sounds a bit too good if you ask me. You're having me on, Crow, you swine.' Mike laughed.

'No, man, honest. You'll see. There's a big cheese coming in at 3.00 p.m. to talk to us.'

'Yeah, OK. Not April the first is it?'

Mike still wasn't sure if Crow was having him on.

'Have you finished with that measuring cylinder? Pass it over, there's a good boy.'

Crow obliged, grinning with satisfaction at Mike's reaction to what really was the truth.

They both separated to carry out their various tasks at different parts of the lab. The job involved a lot of walking about as equipment had been added piecemeal over the years and placed where there was available space, the result of which was a very inefficient layout. On one of Mike's grand tours of the workplace to use a particular piece of testing gear, he was interrupted by one of the Bobs, Big Bob. This Bob was a big burly red-faced chap, in his forties, who liked his whisky and always walked around with his shirt open almost to the waist, summer and winter. With his grey-haired hairy chest exposed, he looked more like a navvy than a technical assistant, and Mike supposed the whisky kept him warm.

'Good news, eh, Mike?'

'Sounds great. Let's hope it's true.'

Big Bob didn't reply, obviously convinced it was good news and simply walked on, smiling and whistling merrily. Probably spend the extra money on better sorts of whiskies, Mike thought rather ungenerously; particularly as he very well might spend some of his money in the same way.

Eventually reaching his destination, Mike found Roy was also working close by.

'Heard the news then?' Roy said, offering Mike a cigarette.

He hadn't seen Roy since 'the event' and was expecting some remark or other. Mike himself didn't think it was his place to make the first move in any conversation on the subject. After all, it had been his wife, in their home, and in case of any after-the-event recriminations it seemed a safer option to say nothing.

'Thanks,' Mike said, taking the offered cigarette and lighting both his and Roy's.

'Yeah, Crow told me. Sounds good if it's true.'

'It won't bother me. I'm leaving anyway.'

'Leaving? Blimey, you've only just started. Where you going?'

'It's a rep job, for a pharmaceutical company. I'll be going around calling on doctors and hospitals. Good job, with a car as well.'

He gave a self-satisfied smirk.

'Well, I'm surprised, Roy. I suppose there will be training, about medical stuff.'

'Oh, yeah, but it's nine to five, no more shift work and no more smelly sticky resins. I hate this shift work lark.'

Mike gave a grunt of agreement.

'When is all this happening?'

'Monday.'

'Monday. Bloody hell, that's quick. What about putting in your notice?'

'I put that in weeks ago, and, of course, I'll be out all day,' he added, giving Mike a knowing look. 'You'll have to keep an eye on Babs for me.' At this remark he gave Mike a long leering sneer. Mike said nothing but took a long drag of his cigarette, and fiddled with the test equipment.

'Oh, yeah, you're going to Julie's I hear. Good looker, eh? You won't get anything there mate. I've tried; I think she's a lesbian. Wasn't interested at all. They haven't any kids, you know. Yeah, she's a lesbian all right, bitch,' he sneered. 'Her old man is a bit odd as well. Wouldn't come over to our place, uh.'

Mike had been surprised at Bob's impassioned comments.

His manner was normally quite laconic and quietly spoken and so Mike just gave a non-committal, 'Oh, right.'

They had both finished their cigarettes at the same time and this seemed to signal a simultaneous parting.

'Right, Roy, see you at break time. You can tell me all about the job then.'

Well, what a day of news this was turning out to be. Mike thought Roy to be an incredibly secretive sort of bloke to have said nothing at all about his pending departure, but then, on reflection, he hadn't ever said much of any consequence anyway. In fact, Mike knew very little about him apart from his abiding interest in sex.

Nothing had been said about the other evening but it had been made plain, although perhaps rather obliquely, that he was free to call on Babs on his own, which Mike conceded to himself would be preferable to having Roy present and he felt a kick of excitement in his stomach, and groin, at the idea of another visit to Babs.

Jan had finished her stint at the hotel at three o'clock and was preparing to get a bus to the community hall for a couple of hours of rehearsals. Rita, her neighbour, was picking the kids up from school and looking after them until Jan got home at around 5.00 p.m. As she left the building she was surprised to see Tony, Julie's husband sitting outside in his car. Tony wound down the car window.

'Want a lift home, O beautiful one? It looks like it's going to snow,' he said in his best flirty manner and smiling broadly.

And indeed the sky certainly looked wintry.

'I'm not going home, kind sir,' Jan said, responding to his nonsense and returning the smile. 'I'm off to rehearsals at the hall.'

'Get in anyway. I'll take you O star of the show.'

At this, Jan laughed again and got in.

It was 3.00 p.m. and, as Crow had promised, the Big Cheese had arrived. The place was hushed except for the humming of various bits of testing machinery. The work-force, including some plant workers and office staff, stood around in silence. The Cheese, a short, pot-bellied, bald chap with a plump shiny pampered face, in his fifties, dressed in an expensive-looking suit, stood by the report sheet rostrum. He spoke with an easygoing confident manner, typical of the successful and wealthy. Nevertheless, what Crow had said seemed right enough. There were to be pay rises and other benefits to bring the pay and conditions in line with the oil industry. It was all fantastic news and a murmur of excitement went through the gathering, and Crow repeatedly gave Mike a dig in the ribs with his elbow as each point was confirmed, as if to say: I told you so.

The meeting over, the small, and now happy, crowd dispersed, grinning inanely at each other as they did so, and with renewed camaraderie and thoughts of how to spend the extra money. Mike couldn't wait to tell Jan the good news.

Janice and her voluntary chauffeur had reached the community hall and Tony parked the car facing a wall and between two other parked cars. In this position he thought it less likely people could see into the car.

'Here we are, as promised, princess,' he murmured, putting on the charm.

As he spoke he lent towards Jan cupping and fondling a breast through her clothes and planting a kiss upon her lips. Although surprised, she didn't pull away and she felt an unfamiliar surge of excitement. She returned the kiss, allowing his hand to move from breast to thigh, briefly. In an unusually confident and firm tone but with a smile, she removed his hand from her leg and pulled away from their embrace.

'Down boy, down. I've got to go. Don't you have any work to get back to? They're waiting for me. I am the star after all,' she said smilingly and with mock air of importance, adding rather ruefully, 'Uh, that will be the day.'

He ignored the remark about him getting back to his work – whatever that was precisely.

'Will I see you before you come to our place on Saturday?'

'Well, I don't know, I'm in the hotel until one o'clock tomorrow – bye I've really got to go. Thanks for the lift, Tony.'

As Tony had predicted, a few flakes of snow had began to fall and Janice dashed into the warmth of the dusty old hall.

'Hi, Jan. You OK? You look all hot and bothered. Are you all right?' enquired Julie and Marie more or less in unison.

Temporarily flustered by bumping into Tony's wife, of all people, and of Tony's attentions, Janice answered with a quick, 'No, no, I'm absolutely fine, Jules. I've been rushing around all day that's all. I'm really all right,' adding, 'It's trying to snow out there.'

'Is it?'

The two women shrieked with childish glee and rushed to the door to investigate, giving Jan time to gather her thoughts. Indeed, she was all right – and aglow. Perhaps aroused was a better description. Her face and down to her lower neckline were flushed blush pink, and her large blue eyes glistened. She had in a way expected him to make a move of some sort; she could tell by the way he looked at her that he fancied her. Janice felt excited by the incident and also a little confused. Morally confused. Although they had been married in church, at the insistence of the parents, she wasn't religious but did think it was wrong to mess with other people's husbands and wives. But then, she reasoned with herself, Mike had been with Babs, although she still hadn't actually asked him outright, so perhaps she could go with Tony – couldn't she?

'It's not snowing much, Jan,' said Julie disappointedly. 'It could be a white Christmas though. That would be great, wouldn't it?'

'It would be nice,' Jan replied in a rather distant tone, her brain still contemplating the possibilities of Tony.

'Here's Bill, Hi Bill.' Marie gave a limp wave towards the entrance. We'd better get started. You know what he's like if we mess about,' she added quietly and conspiratorially.

Jan and Julie mumbled their agreement and Jan promised herself that she would have to continue her fantasy at another time.

10.00 p.m. and the shift ended and Mike drove home rather more enthusiastically then he had driven into work. The snow hadn't really come to much and there was just a light covering on the roads so he got home with ease.

As soon as he got into the front door, Mike, almost shouting, called out, 'Great news, Darl.'

He now rarely called her Darl and Jan hadn't said it for a while.

'Shh, you'll wake the kids. What is it?'

Mike told her the good news. Jan too was greatly pleased about the extra money.

'We'll be able to get some things for the house now and buying Christmas presents will be easier,' Mike enthused.

'Choosing Christmas presents for your mother and sister is never easy,' Jan retorted in a more practical tone.

'Yeah, well, you know what I mean.'

Jan liked him in this boyish energetic mode and would have liked to give him a little hug and a kiss, but held back in case he got the wrong idea. Instead, she got up and headed for the kitchen to prepare him something to eat and drink.

'Yes, I know what you mean.' So saying, she gave him a light touch on the shoulder as a substitute for the kiss. 'What do you fancy to eat?'

'Fried bacon and baked beans would be nice – to celebrate.'

'Your wish is my command, sir,' Jan said with a smile and left the room.

In what seemed to be the distant past, a happy event such as this would have meant an almost certain chance of being followed by a goodly cuddle and sex in bed. But Mike was now reluctant even to mention it in case the seemingly fragile but reasonably safe relationship they now had would be broken. In his book, it wasn't an ideal situation, far from it. But it appeared that as long as sex was never mentioned their life together would somehow roll along reasonably enough. Mike was saddened by the prospect of this con-clusion. However, they had grown apart, and they had both stopped saying, 'I love you'. He no longer actively thought of silly little actions or words to enhance their days. He didn't make so many jokes, or come up behind her at the kitchen sink and fondle her breasts or playfully press his groin against her whilst she was up to her elbows in suds. Watching her undress and lying beside her in bed, but unable to touch intimately, was agonising at times, but it was better than no marriage at all. What was the point of conflict, of rows? He detested rowing. He wanted them to be happy, he wanted to stay with Jan and the children. If this meant sacrificing sex with Jan, then so be it.

Jan too had things on her mind. Back home after the

rehearsals she had busied herself seeing to the children, and doing 101 other chores. But her mind had been elsewhere. In fact, she was thinking far more than she was used to, and was now juggling many thoughts at once: the household chores, rehearsals, Mike and now the Tony business. His tentative car-park groping had excited her imaginative processes immensely. If she hadn't had the kids around when she got home, she would have indulged herself upstairs. However, it wasn't really about actually having sex with Tony. It was the attention, the fantasised possibilities of the unknown that thrilled her. Sex certainly has some oblique ways of expressing itself. But would it really be so different with him than with Mike?

The next day at work more details of the changes began to filter through to the workforce. Probably more exciting than the pay rises themselves, was the idea of a new shift system, which was named, rather alluringly, Continental. It meant basically a shorter shift week and more changes within it. Mike had been reading the proposals avidly so was considered to be the expert on the subject. And at break time, Crow, between mouthfuls of a pork pie, asked Mike for a breakdown of the information he couldn't be bothered to read himself.

'How is this Continental thingy going to work then?'

'As I read it, it will be two afternoons, two mornings and two nights starting on the last day of mornings, if you see what I mean, then two off, plus one extra day off a month.'

'Christ, man, sounds bloody complicated to me. We'll be going around in circles and disappearing up our own arses.'

'Well,' said Old Navy Bill, taking a leisurely puff of his pipe and continuing in an accentuated posh tone, 'I shall not be disappearing up MY anus.'

They erupted into laughter at this and the matter was dropped and replaced by more intimate one-to-one chat.

'Oh, yeah, Susan wants to know if you can up to our

place for nosh and that, before the Christmas madness starts.'

' "And that" sounds a bit dangerous, Crow,' Mike replied thoughtfully, his fingers remembering Susan's soft thighs, and he gave Crow a knowing look.

'Eh.' Crow looked blank at first then realised the private joke and giggled. 'On second thoughts, I don't think there will be any of "that" on the menu.'

'Yeah, I should think it will be all right, matey, but I'll ask Jan anyway. Oh yes, I've got some news for you. Roy is leaving.'

'Bloody hell man. Who told you that? And where is he anyway, I haven't seen him.'

'He did, yesterday. He's got the shift off.'

'Bloody hell,' Crow repeated, stunned by what he considered to be good news. 'Never liked the weird bugger anyway,' Crow concluded, and lit up a cigarette, and the room fell silent.

Mike was beginning privately to agree with Crow. Roy was certainly different from the other people in Mike's small circle of friends and acquaintances. He couldn't put his finger on precisely what was different about him but there was something. If Mike were honest with himself he would have admitted that he didn't much like Roy either, but wanted to keep in with him so that he could get his hands, as it were, on Babs.

Thinking about Babs lead him to ponder the prospects that might occur at Julie's. The evening visit was only days away and he hadn't yet sorted the days off he needed for the event. He wasn't really expecting anything to happen, particularly as he hadn't met her husband. And, of course, Jan would be there as well. Perhaps he was odd, as Roy had said, but then Roy's outburst sounded more like sour grapes than fact, because he hadn't had his way with Julie. Mike also concluded that the wife-swapping business was very time-consuming and not as convenient as sex within the home. Of course, he hadn't actually swapped anything – yet.

The shift came to an end and Mike and Crow set off for home. Crow had very recently bought an old car, a very old car, and it spent most of its time in some garage or other being repaired. This was such a day and Mike had, naturally enough, offered to take him home.

'Man, it's a bit bloody nippy out here.'

'Yeah, sure is. I think were going to get more snow.' Mike opened the car and started the engine. 'Soon have some heat.'

'Great, this is better than hanging about for the bus,' Crow said, rubbing his hands for warmth.

'Any time, matey, and home we go,' Mike said, manoeuvring the car out through the factory gates onto the open road.

'Home to hot cocoa and sex. Or is it hot sex and cocoa,' said Mike cheerfully and with bravado, knowing full well neither was coming his way.

'Fat chance, mate,' Crow responded gloomily. 'Since she's had the kid she's gone off proper sex. She's gone all clitty.'

Mike was surprised at Crow's remarks and never dreamed that Crow would have sex problems, and certainly wouldn't admit any of his to Crow. Strangly enough, even though they were close friends, they rarely had the opportunity for one-to-one talk and Mike found Crow's predicament instantly depressing, not only because it destroyed his image of Crow as a trouble-free spirit, but it also reminded him of his own disappointment with Jan. But at least Crow and Susan were doing something sexual together. But he really didn't understand exactly what 'all clitty' meant. He would have to play this carefully.

'I know what you mean, mate, the more I think about it

the more I think women are a separate species. They're a bloody mystery.'

This approach seemed to work because Crow carried on talking.

'Yeah, you can say that again. She doesn't want the real thing, she just lets me rub her off. I get all ready for it and then she expects me to do the same with myself. Bloody hell,' he said dejectedly. 'Says she's decided that she doesn't trust the pill, or johnnies, and doesn't want any more kids. I think she just making excuses.'

'Yeah, they all get a bit odd after they've had kids,' Mike said sympathetically and still wondering about the 'clitty' bit. He had got an O level in human biology so knew where and what the clitoris was and assumed that's what Crow meant. But why would any woman want that rubbed instead of the real thing inside? In their courting days any petting they had indulged in, involved vigorous finger attention inside that 'magic cavern'. And he had always believed Jan had enjoyed his ministrations. Not that she had ever said so or ever reciprocated with any petting for him, but he thought that was normal. Mind you, he sometimes got so excited on those occasions that he would come in his trousers, so it wasn't all bad news.

God, Crow was 19 years old and seemed to know something he didn't. Mike's ego didn't like that. After all, he was the one involved in the extraordinary up-to-date wife swapping, and he resolved to find out more – somehow. He certainly wasn't going to ask Crow for any details, and obviously he couldn't discuss it with Jan. So he supposed it was back to the library, unless of course someone else could teach him more . . .

The next day Janice finished work at her usual time and on her way out found, not unexpectedly this time, Tony waiting for her.

'Rehearsals today?'

'No, I'm off home.'

'I'll give you a lift if you like, princess, I'm going that way.'

'OK that will be nice. It's freezing out here, and I've been on my feet all day.'

'You need a lie down.' He paused, giving her a knowing look and, smiling, then added, 'Put your feet up, rest,' just in case she thought he was being too suggestive and pushy.

He was a charmer.

Jan got the message all right, and a thrill of excitement mixed with apprehension passed through her body. Her mind racing along well ahead of his, possibilities and problems spun around her brain. 'Oh God, my stomach. Julie's not marked like me, it will put him off me – he won't like me and I'm fat. I'll keep my clothes on. I'll think of something. Should I be thinking like this? Why should I want to do this? I'm happy as I am. Am I? And besides, what about Julie, she's my friend. I don't want any unpleasantness.'

'Here we are, home sweet home.'

She wished he hadn't said that. It was one of Mike's sayings.

But she found herself asking, 'Do you fancy a cup of coffee?'

'Thought you'd never ask.'

He grinned.

Janice showed Tony into the sitting room, and went into the kitchen to make the drinks. The drinks made, they sat side by side on the small settee, their bodies touching in the confined space. Each could feel the body heat of the other. Their drinks lay untouched on the low table as they talked – about nothing at all. Then he turned towards Jan, placing a hand on her thigh and kissing her on the lips. Soon his hand was travelling unhindered under her skirt and Jan lifted herself slightly, allowing the skirt greater movement upwards towards her waist. Tony's hand was now allowed to pull the knickers to one side. He touched and stroked and Jan gasped with excitement as he gently parted the lips, and one, then two fingers slipped easily inside her. He returned to his stroking and rubbing and quickly brought a shudder and groan of satisfaction from Jan. He made no attempt to satisfy himself by entering her, and simply smiled, gave a little kiss, and returned to his coffee, now rather cold. A real charmer indeed.

Jan straightened her clothes and then she too reached for her coffee and they both sat as though nothing at all unusual had happened.

'Are you and Mike still coming over on Saturday night?'

'Oh yes, of course we are,' Jan said enthusiastically, her flushed face slowly returning to normal. 'About half past seven Julie said.'

'Probably be a late night, how do you cope with the kids?'

'Oh Mike's mum will look after them. They can stay with her for the night. They'll be fine.'

'Righto, princess, I'm off now, see you soon.'

He gave her a light kiss on the cheek and was gone. Jan, however, was still somewhat aroused and headed upstairs, ostensibly – to change . . .

Later that afternoon, with the children delivered safely back home by her good neighbour, Rita, Jan went about her chores with her head reliving the earlier events. Her out of character experience had proved from her point of view successful and she was in a buoyant and confident mood. And she was pleased that it hadn't gone any further and that her body had remained unviewed. Indeed, even her conscience was clear. After all, she reasoned with herself, being touched wasn't as bad as allowing him to go all the way and with her secretive nature she had no intention of saying anything to Mike. She had been mightily impressed by Tony's ability to bring her satisfaction, although of course it wasn't the 'real' thing and was now wondering if he would be as good in that department as well, not that she was anxious in going all the way with Tony. If she did, it would be more out of curiosity rather than with any expectation of true pleasure, and was quite happy with the result of the day's events. Jan also wondered why Mike had never shown an interest in doing what Tony had done so easily. It didn't cross her mind that it might have been the particular situation, and not necessarily the man alone, which had brought about the ecstatic pleasure.

After putting the children to bed, Jan spent the evening making Christmas lists, one for cards, one for presents. If Mike could get a lift or the bus to work the next day she planned taking the car into town and do some serious shopping. The days were going by at their usual frantic rate and Christmas was approaching rapidly and there was always so much to do, and on Saturday they were going to Julie's and Tony's. At this thought she felt a little wave of excitement run through her. At 10.30 p.m. Mike got home from his labours and another day came to an end.

10

Saturday night arrived and all the usual personal preparations were made in earnest. The children had been deposited at Mike's mum's for the night, which they enjoyed immensely, knowing they would be spoiled rotten. Jan took longer than usual to choose her outfit for the evening and the heap of cast aside clothes on the bed grew by the minute. As she stomped about in her underwear, complete with stockings and suspenders, he watched, enjoying the sexy sight with frustrated lust.

Mike himself had no such trouble with his attire. Because of his reluctance to fashion, Jan told him what to put on, which suited him down to the ground and saved him the bother. Jan eventually made her mind up and opted for a dress which he liked to see her in. He called it brown-coloured, but probably had some other proper exotic title. It showed off her breasts and waist to perfection. She looked gorgeous.

As they busied themselves getting ready, each, unbeknown to the other, had their own agenda running through their heads. Jan, slightly nervous in case Julie had found out about her and Tony's brief erotic contact, and Mike for his part was simply wondering what the food was going to be like. He didn't think anything naughty would happen, not with her husband and Jan there; so tasty food and plenty of it was Mike's next priority.

The house, situated close to the town centre, was found easily enough. A large Edwardian terraced three-storey place was similar to Roy's, but not as big. But for two people it was huge and Jan and Mike were quietly envious of all that space.

Mike hadn't met Julie's husband so didn't know what to expect. Come to that, he hardly knew Julie either and so was a little apprehensive as to the evening's prospects and he began to remember why he didn't like parties. So he ushered Jan ahead of him as a buffer against the unknown as they entered through the large half-glazed front door.

'Hi, Julie.'

'Jan, come on in, and Mike.'

Once in the hall, music could be heard from somewhere deep inside the house, and a man appeared.

'Tony, this is Mike,' Julie said, flashing those blue eyes of hers at Mike.

'Hello, Tony.'

Mike held out a hand which Tony shook a little too vigorously for Mike's liking. Some men are like that. They think handshaking is some sort of competition to see who can crush the other's hand first.

'Come on in, Mike. What do fancy to drink?'

Tony more or less ignored Jan who was already deep in conversation with Julie and led Mike into the sitting room where the source of the music, an up-to-date stereo record player, was situated. Books were stacked on shelves and tops of cupboards and the room was scruffily homely, complete with an open fire, and Mike began to relax as an array of bottles, laid out on a side table, came into view.

'You won't go thirsty here,' he said, smiling at Mike's reaction to the hoard of alcoholic goodies.

Tony seemed affable enough and not a bit like he thought he would look like. In fact, in Mike's eyes he looked like a bit like Benny Hill, slightly shorter than Mike and a lot heavier, and he wondered why Jan found him attractive. The girls soon joined them, drinks were chosen and dispensed and they all settled themselves into chairs of their choice. Even though the choice seemed random, it ended up with Mike next to Julie and Jan next to Tony.

'So you work in a laboratory at the plastics' place that stinks half the town out, Mike?' Tony asked.

'Yep, 'fraid so.'

'His clothes stink too,' Jan said.

'Well, someone has to do it,' Mike said, sighing with mock dedication. 'What would you do without your plastic buckets and polythene sheeting? And car brakes?'

'That's true,' said Julie thoughtfully, adding, 'do you make buckets then?'

Mike gave a little laugh and thought, was she serious?

'No, nothing is made on site. We only make the raw materials. Other firms make the goods. I work in the control lab.'

Julie looked blank, but didn't pursue the subject. Mike was beginning to think she was a little bit thick.

'Car brakes? Are they made of plastic?' Tony enquired with interest.

'Sort of. Brake linings are actually made from cashew nut shell oil, asbestos and some other bits and pieces. The shells are crushed and the oil sent to our place and processed and sent out to the makers.'

'Good God, brakes made from nut shells, I didn't know that – that's amazing,' Tony responded with enthusiasm, as though he wanted to know more.

However, Julie seemed bored and interrupted the proceedings by getting up and crossing to the drinks' table. Mike was pleased by the break in the conversation. He didn't particularly like talking about work and, to his ears, it had started to sound like a lecture.

'Any one for a drink?'

Julie smiled.

Across town Roy was greeting another visitor.

'Graham, come in. You found the place all right?'

'Couldn't miss it really.'

'We're on the second floor. Carol not with you?'

'No. Couldn't get a babysitter.'

'That's OK, perhaps next time.'

'Nice place, Roy, big too.'

'We don't notice it.'

'Here we are. Go on in, Graham. Barbara is waiting to meet you.'

'I'll have another whisky and American, if that's OK.'

'Of course it is, you can have anything you want.'

Julie gave him a big grin full of meaning and Mike shot a glance at Jan to see if she had noticed the innuendo. Jan hadn't, and was chatting to Tony in a very relaxed manner. Of course Janice already knew Tony, so this seemed normal enough.

Mike settled back in his chair, already enveloped in a warm glow from his unfamiliar whisky drinking. This is OK he thought. A real fire, and whisky by the tumblerfull. Yes, this is OK.

'Do you like Tom Jones? I love him, he's great – and a Welshman – *Cymru am byth* – Wales for ever. "Delilah" is his best, oh and "Help Yourself", that's great as well, came out in August.'

So saying, in her usual high-speed breathless way, and not waiting for an answer, Julie put the record on and turned up the volume. Was Julie already drunk or what? Jan and Mike gave each other a glance of surprise at her behaviour. Jan was used to Julie's frenetic manner but tonight she seemed more excitable than usual.

'Turn it down a bit, love.' You'll have the neighbours complaining,' Tony said with a laugh.

'You're all spoilsports,' Julie said in a girly voice and with pouting lips.

Turning down the volume, she slumped back down next to Mike.

'Do you speak Welsh, Jules? All that *Cymru am byth*, stuff?' asked Jan, trying to get back to more usual topics.

'Of course, I was born in Llanelli,' Julie replied proudly.

'Our kids do, and Mike, a bit,' Jan continued. 'His grandmother was a Welsh speaker. That's why we sent them to the Welsh school, and because they start at three years old. I'm hopeless, but we're both trying to learn more. Aren't we, Mike?'

'Yeah, when I get the time.'

God, Julie's mad, and Welsh, Mike considered through the whisky haze.

'You're not one of those Welsh Nationalists are you, Jules? You know, blowing up water pipes and stuff like that. I can just see you in the Free Wales Army uniform,' Mike said mischievously.

'No, of course not, but the English shouldn't have Welsh water for free,' she replied vehemently, her unusual forget-me-not blue eyes sparkling with passion, reminding Mike of one of the reasons he fancied her.

'More drinks everyone?' Tony said, striding purposefully to the drinks' table, 'and who's ready for some food?'

It seemed that Roy was used to taking over the duty of the hostess, and of distracting Julie from her ranting.

'How about it Jules? I'm starving.'

So far Mike had had two large drinks well ahead of the others who were just finishing their first. But he didn't refuse another, believing the food would quickly soak up the booze. He too was hungry. Julie left to sort out the food and without her the three-way conversation settled into the cheerful, bland, middle of the party sort.

'That's it, Graham. Give it to her. Give it to her hard. Go on, she likes it rough. Shag her good and hard.'

Roy's eyes glinted with wild delight, his body trembling with excitement . . .

'Right, my turn – get off her.'

'Lovely meal, Jules,' Jan said appreciatively.

'Yeah, great, thanks', Mike added.

The evening had moved along very nicely and they were all in good spirits, Mike in particular, as he was now on his fourth very large drink. The meal over, they settled back in their previous sitting positions, and the evening continued.

By about midnight the mood of the gathering had began to change to a mellow quieter tone, including the choice of music. Mike had stopped drinking, realising with some difficulty that he was well over his alcohol limit, and was trying to stabilise his stomach and head by sneaking a drink of water at each visit to the lavatory. He didn't want to disgrace himself by being ill. It could have been his fuddled brain but to him the others appeared remarkably sober. He knew Jan didn't usually drink a lot for fear of putting on weight. But as for Tony and Julie, he had no idea what they had been consuming or what they could take.

Sex hadn't been mentioned once, but Mike hadn't expected it to be. He hardly knew these two people – not like Crow and Susan.

By this time Julie was sitting very close to Mike and occasionally her hand brushed across his thigh, not that Mike in his inebriated state had really noticed.

Another hour of party time had passed by and on one of his return visits from his water drinking expeditions he found the room empty, except for Julie.

'Bed time, come on,' she said, taking his hand and leading him out into the hall and up the stairs. He assumed she was taking him to wherever Jan and he were going to sleep for the night. But on entering the bedroom there was no sign of Jan – or Tony. Mike didn't want to lose his sophisticated persona but inwardly he was stunned. Was Jan with Tony? Christ, that is unbelievable. My Jan with another man – bloody hell! And me with Julie. Mike didn't have time to decide whether he liked this situation or not, because Julie was undressing, smiling and gyrating in a half-hearted strip-tease manner. Through the whisky haze Mike was mildly amused at her amateur attempts at eroticism and thought once again she was a bit of a nut case.

'Do you like my panties, Mike? Look, they've got the days of the week embroidered on them.'

She moved closer to the bed upon which Mike had slumped.

'Look, can you see it?'

As she thrust her hips forward to give a better reading distance, the movement also accentuated the mound between her thighs and Mike felt the first kick of excitement of the evening.

'Um, very nice, Jules.'

The black knickers did indeed have Saturday night embroidered in white letters on the front.

'I've got a pair for every day of the week, all different colours. White virginal ones for Sunday.' She grinned and giggled.

'Very nice, Jules,' he repeated, reaching out and running his hand over the prominent mound as he spoke.

'Don't be naughty,' she said, moving away from the bed a little and continuing her strip-tease performance, taking off her bra and the Saturday knickers and staggering about a bit as she tried to step out of them in a sexy way.

'Bet you haven't seen a ginger one before.' She grinned, regaining her balance, and again thrusting her hips forward and running her fingers through the triangle of hair.

'It's really nice, Jules, and lots of it. I like hairy ones,' Mike slurred, the whisky taking its toll and his choice of words totally inadequate.

He was annoyed with himself for drinking so much. But how was he to know how the evening was going to turn out? And part of his mind was distracted by Jan and Tony. What the hell was going on there?

Between the bouts of strip-tease, Mike had slowly taken off his own clothes and climbed under the sheets and was, eventually, joined by Julie. Although he was far from his normal self and not really in any state for sex, Mike had no intention of missing out on experiencing another woman. He made a move to get on top of Julie but she had other ideas.

Taking his hand she placed it between her legs, showing him what she wanted.

She was soon making low moaning noises and fondling and squeezing her own breasts, pulling and stretching her nipples until Mike thought she might screw them off all together. And the moans becoming louder as her body writhed. He really liked the sounds of pleasure she made, something he hadn't heard quite like this before, and he found the whole scene new and exciting. But it seemed to him an inordinately long time before he achieved the result Jules wanted, and overall he hadn't enjoyed it too much – all that rubbing. It was hard work and his arm ached.

'That was very very nice,' she said with a contented sigh. 'I knew you'd be good at it. I was right wasn't I?'

She gave a grin, like a cat with cream.

'Now it's your turn, I'm all yours . . .'

11

'Mummy, Mummy,' Mandy shouted joyfully, running up to Jan and Mike as they entered the sitting room at his mother's house.

'Dad, Dad, come an' look at my new Tonka tractor Aunty Marion got me,' David said excitedly.

David was already beginning to grow away from Jan and more or less ignored her, preferring to talk toy tractors with his dad. The children had been too engrossed in their playthings scattered over the floor to have heard their beloved parents arriving at grandma's so were especially surprised. Although they enjoyed their visits, and the gross spoiling they received, they were always glad to leave, probably for the same reasons as their parents – the constant brainwashing about correct social etiquette and the like.

'Did you have a good party? You must have, it's ten o'clock.'

'Yes, great, Mum. Sorry it's so late,' replied Mike.

'Were there lots of people and lots of food?'

This was his mother at her interrogative worse.

'Well, eh, um, quite a few.'

He looked towards Jan, who was playing on the floor with the children, hoping for support, but she kept her head down, avoiding his gaze, leaving him to cope with the inquisitor.

'Yeah, food was great,' he continued.

He thought it best not to say that there had only been the four of them, just in case she would think it was an odd sort of party, and why they had to stay overnight. Thankfully, just as his mother drew breath for her next question, Marion came into the room with a tray of coffees and kiddie drinks.

'Hi, Marion, been spoiling the kids again. It's nearly Christmas too,' said Mike, pleased at the reprieve, even if only temporarily.

'Oh, it doesn't matter. I'm sure Santa will find some more toys.'

This was something else that annoyed Jan immensely. They would buy things for the children, clothes as well as toys, without checking whether or not she approved, or that she might have already bought for them.

'Do you want to stay for a cooked meal with us? Not in a rush to go home are you?' Marion asked. Without waiting for a response, Mike's mother decided for them by getting up, heading for the kitchen and saying, 'That's settled then, I'll get it started. You don't want to be getting home late with the children.'

Jan was secretly pleased. She hadn't fancied going home and cooking.

Later after the meal of roast chicken, including some of Marion's homegrown Brussels sprouts, of which she was extremely proud, Jan and Mike decided to take the kids for a runabout on the winter-deserted beach before eventually reaching home. As soon as they were through the front door Mandy, obviously wound up by his sister, slipped into early Christmas mode.

'When is Father Christmas coming, Mummy? Is he coming tonight?' Mandy asked, her little face furrowed with anxiety and looking more frightened than pleased at the prospect of a strange man with a bushy beard coming into her room in the middle of the night.

'No, not yet, sweetheart. You've got to be good for a long time yet or he won't bring you any presents,' Janice replied, picking her up and giving her a hug and a kiss.

'I'm always good,' David stated emphatically.

'You're both very good. Did you have a nice time at Grandmas?'

'Yeah, we had ice cream, and sweets and we watched telly in the night,' David stated, happily reliving the treats.

And it sounded as though they stayed up later than normal.

'We had to have a bath – I didn't want to,' David said indignantly.

'You weren't naughty for Grandma were you?'

Jan suspected he might have been a bit rebellious.

'No, we wasn't, Mum,' Mandy and David said almost in unison.

'That's all right then. Off you go now and get ready for bed. Daddy will be up in a minute and read you a story. Night night, my lovelies.'

Janice kissed them both and the children headed gleefully up the stairs.

Christmas was indeed looming close. Janice had completed most of the present buying. All that remained was, as usual, Mike's mum and sister. They seemed to have everything they wanted but were so generous with their gifts that Jan and Mike had to stretch their brains and think of something appropriate – and affordable. And then the kids had to have their day out and visit Santa's grotto. The nearest big town, well in fact it had recently become a city, was Aberdod, about ten miles away, hardly a big trek, but they shopped there so rarely it was a big outing when they did so.

'All settled now but they 're wound up like watch springs and we've got another twenty odd days to go yet. I bet mum and Marion got them all worked up about Christmas.'

This conversation was so normal, so everyday, yet last night they had both been involved in something so abnormal. Neither of them ever thought that in such a short time their lives would be so changed, and each was trying to evaluate exactly which reaction, and what conclusions, they should make and convey to the other. None of the participants in whatever went on behind those closed doors, were, for want of a better word, common or lacking in social and personal morals. And in a way, perhaps it was a similar situation to Mike's ideas about people overcoming their fears or prejudices in order to step into other extraordinary worlds, to have new experiences in order to know themselves, to learn or simply to enjoy, although Tony and Julie seemed very relaxed and indiffent with the whole business.

Breakfast time at Tony and Julie's had been strange but not especially strained. A cup of coffee and a slice of toast was all most of them could manage, particularly Mike who, being unaware that anything unusual was going to occur, had drunk the most, well unusual for Mike and Jan, that is. Whether or not such evenings were usual to the hosts was totally unknown to them. Perhaps it was just a one-off event and not really connected with the vogue of wife swapping – except as an excuse to experiment. And they seemed, to Mike at least, just average people like themselves. Perhaps it was as though each was avoiding any recognition of what had happened. But, although any eye contact had been brief, there hadn't been any real evidence of uncomfortable embarrassment.

Mike, however, was still mystified as to Jan's behaviour. Had she had sex with Tony? She must have. The idea was incredible and he wasn't sure he was happy about it. Did it mean that her interest for sex was revived? Maybe, but he still didn't have the nerve to make any waves by asking her, certainly not now, not today, even though he longed to know what she was thinking. But because she hadn't ever asked him what he had done with Babs and now Julie, he now supposed he had to follow the same path and ask no questions.

The more Mike relived the situation the more he felt he had been through some sort of test and that the others involved were each in the know as to what was to take place, but, he reasoned, that couldn't really be the case. No doubt that in a few days' time, when his body had recovered from the booze, he would be viewing all this differently. He had certainly learned something new with Julie. Crow's Susan wasn't an exception after all. But it was a pity Mike couldn't tell him as much. He might ask too many awkward questions about how and where he had discovered the information. So something good had come out of the evening and, apart from a few alcohol-related false starts, he had eventually made it with Jules, much to his delight. Now here they were, 7.00 on a Sunday evening, back home and putting the kids to bed, and everything as normal as Yorkshire pud, as Mike's grandmother would have said. Although, at this point in time they seemed strangely more distant from each other than ever. And in their little sitting room, in their little house, all was quiet.

'Pete', Roy exclaimed, surprised to see him on the doorstep on a Sunday evening but nevertheless pleased.

'Well, I was at a bit of a loose end so I thought I'd call like, to see you. And Barbara of course.'

Peter spoke with hesitation, and he smelt of booze.

'Of course you would,' Roy said in sneering tone. 'Come on up. I'm sure Babs will be really happy to see you again.'

'Oh great,' Pete replied enthusiastically. 'I was hoping you'd say that.'

Barbara would, in fact, be far from happy.

They both were tired from the exertions of the previous evening activities and in bed and asleep by 10.00 p.m. Which was just as well because Mike had to be in work next day by 8.00 a.m. The new shift system was due to begin on Monday morning and Mike's shift had been chosen to start the ball rolling. It meant that they would lose out on rest days, but someone had to begin the system and they would be paid well for the inconvenience and lack of a break. It meant he would be doing two mornings and then a night shift on the second day of mornings, all a bit confusing at first, for him and Jan and the kids, but in the long run it could be better than the old system. Only time would tell.

He felt refreshed and energetic as he set of to begin work. His doubts and concerns about Jan's activities with Tony were in better perspective and, in fact, the feelings of social superiority and sophistication, which he had after the Bab's and Roy evening, had returned. Indeed, he believed he had the best of both worlds. The security and, yes, the love he hoped deep down they still had, and now, the massive sexual freedom with other women. It was all too good to be true.

With Mike in work and the children in school, Jan too was in reflective mode as she went about the usual Monday morning activites. Jan, like her mother and countless other women, did the clothes washing on a Monday. Although Jan had a second-hand twin-tub washing machine and could do the wash at any time, she still preferred to get it over with early in the week regardless of the weather. Mind you, in winter it took nigh on a week to dry, and often any area near the gas fires would be festooned with damp clothes.

As she busied herself with the chores of the day she too was thinking about Tony and the events of Saturday night. Being with another man in such circumstances had reminded her all too vividly of her doubts about marriage. Even on the wedding day itself she hadn't been sure it was what she wanted. She had certainly wanted to get away from home. Her two older sisters had married and were long gone, and as a very late child, Jan was left with an irritable mother who was going through the change, and a loving but fairly strict father, not a palatable mix for a young woman anxious to experience life, independence and the freedom from being told what to do all of the time.

As regards sex, she had, from the day she discovered the pleasure of self-induced orgasms, believed she was unique and odd for doing such a thing, and so the lack of self-confidence had begun. She had come close to trying intercourse with other men before she met Mike, just to see if she was 'normal', but fear of pregnancy and perhaps having to marry them put her off the idea. But Mike had seemed different from these other men and a safer bet if anything went wrong and she became pregnant. Even so, after a few quickie sessions with Mike, and the subsequent disappointments, she had easily persuaded him it would be better if they waited until they were married – the rest you know. So her selfishness, if it could be called that, was in marrying Mike in the first place, and not explaining to him her doubts and worries.

Mike had been the more intense and enthusiastic of the two, wanting to know her every thought and feeling, and struggling to explain all his, which Jan, with her taciturn nature, had found extremely wearing at times. His endless quizzing as to what penetration felt like and what her orgasm was like for her was an especially difficult question to answer when with him she wasn't experiencing one anyhow. But Mike assumed all was well and for Mike it was simple. Two people said they loved each other and then lots of sex would ensue. So marriage for him meant perfection in sexual terms, and in general living as well, for he too wanted to get away from his mother and sister.

However, for Jan, the night with Tony had been a surprise to her as well. She knew Julie was a bit scatty but didn't think she would go in for that sort of carry on. Just how wrong can you be? He had often joked in the hotel bar that he was free to do as he liked with other women – 'now and then'. But Jan hadn't believed him, and put it down to booze talk, but the events that night seemed to prove him right. The encounter, however, had not been great, exciting but not satisfying. He had dispensed, with what she liked best and, if she had ever thought size was a factor in her dissatisfaction, then she had now discounted it. Tony was much smaller than Mike – down there. In truth, she found men's 'equipment' as she called it, ugly and ludicrous, and likened it to a male turkey's neck, a strange comparison which used to give Mike a laugh and he would then go around for half the day making gobbling noises. But she really didn't want to repeat the event with Tony and hoped he felt the same. Overall though, Jan wasn't irretrievably despondent about the event and Tony seemed unaffected by her ugly body, and, in fact, she was feeling quite confident. And as Mike didn't seem to care what she did, she would continue, for a while at least, to follow Mike's lead.

12

'So how much is this one?'

'Four hundred and fifty pounds, sir, very nice piano indeed.'

'I should say so,' muttered Mike under his breath. What the hell am I doing in this place, Four hundred and fifty quid? That's half a year's pay. Still, wouldn't get it in the house anyway.

The shop assistant, sensing Mike's obvious shocked state, moved him along the row of open-mouthed beasts to a smaller, less hungry looking model.

'This, sir, is the cheapest at a hundred and seventy eight pounds ten shillings.'

Why the ten shillings Mike thought? Who cares about ten shillings when you're forking out £178 – mad.

'Of course, it's only six and a half octaves,' the assistant remarked a little disdainfully and Mike thought, how many of these octi things do you need anyway?

'What does that mean, exactly?'

'Well, sir, a normal piano has eight octaves, but this one is perfectly adequate for average use.' He emphasised the "average". 'Yes, indeed, a very nice instrument.'

'Yes, OK I'll have it.'

What, are you mad? Did I just say that, oh God what am I doing? With the interest that's £242 10s over the next four years. Mike's stomach lurched with momentary panic, and then relaxed, realising it would only be £4 13s 4d per month. I'm having a pay rise soon and we can always sell it if I can't pay for it, he reasoned. He could be rather impulsive at times.

'Will that be cash, sir?' The assistant paused for a second, taking in Mike's glazed expression, before adding, 'Or hire purchase?'

The hire-purchase paperwork complete and deposit paid, Mike dashed back to the car park and home. He had left work a bit earlier than normal and rushed into Aberdod town centre, thinking that if he was really lucky he would be home about half past two, and Jan would be none the wiser. The piano was to be a huge surprise on Christmas Day. Her parents had an old piano, and at one time had offered it to Jan. But it was really a bit too big for their little place. But whenever they visited them Jan would tinkle away at it but it wasn't convenient to go there every time she wanted to rehearse a song, or just fancied playing. Not only that, but he wanted to show Jan that despite the odd way their life was going, he still loved her, whatever that meant in the circumstances. Secreting the thing was another problem, but he had chatted to Mr Brown, the shopkeeper, who owned the empty shop on the end of the terrace, and he'd agreed Mike could have it delivered and stored there until Christmas. All Mike had to do now was arrange with Keith his neighbour, Rita's husband, to give him a hand pushing it up the street and into the house on Christmas Eve – he just hoped it wouldn't be raining, or snowing. It was brand new after all.

'How did the new shift go this morning?'

'Well, just as normal really. Tomorrow will be odd though. Going back in to do a night shift.'

'I'm out to rehearsals tonight. Is that OK? About half six?'

'Yeah, of course. I'll see to the kids. Coffee ready? I'm gasping for a cuppa and a fag.'

112

'Were you busy then?'

'Rushing about a bit, yeah.'

He smiled a secret smile to himself. He was really looking forward to Christmas and Jan's big surprise.

'Dad, are you going to read us a story?' David enquired, his head lost somewhere in the jumper he was trying to get off.

'Let me help. Of course, I usually do, don't I?'

'And can I have *John and Janet*, Daddy?' Mandy chipped in.

'You can if you sit still long enough.'

Mike laughed.

''Cos Mum said we mustn't nag you,' Dave continued.

'Did she now?' Mike laughed. 'Well that's very nice of her.'

'Daddy, will you help me as well?' said little Mandy who was in an even bigger knot with her clothes.

God, he loved these kids. They were so happy, so exhilarating and Mandy had that special brand of female strength and energy.

'Come here, let me sort you out, sweetheart, you're all tied up like a parcel.'

David giggled.

'You are funny, Dad.'

'I don't want to be a parcel,' whimpered Mandy.

Now it was Mike's turn to giggle.

Eventually Mike settled down by the gas fire with the television on and a book in his hand, with a coffee and a cigarette, half-reading, half-watching. It was about 7.30 p.m. when there was a rapping on the front door. Random callers were very rare, and to Mike, annoying. More rapping. 'OK OK,' Mike shouted cheerfully but muttering, 'is the bloody house on fire or what?'

'Roy and Babs?' Mike said with disbelief, as he opened the door. 'Shouldn't you be at rehearsals, Roy?'

113

'On my way now. Is it OK if Babs waits here for me to come back? We've been visiting relatives and left a bit late and I haven't got time to go back home now.'

His voice faded away as he waited for a reaction from Mike whilst Barbara stood beside him with head bowed.

'Uh, well, yeah fine. Come on in, Babs. Haven't seen you for ages.'

Mike was taken aback by this sudden visitation but couldn't be impolite.

'Right, I'm off. See you later.'

He gave his usual self-satisfied grin and was gone.

'Do you fancy a cup of coffee, tea?'

'OK, coffee would be nice.'

She smiled. He definitely liked her mouth, very nice.

'Right, I'll put the kettle on. Sit down, relax. I won't be a minute.'

Babs sat back and began to look less tense and worried. Mike soon returned with two steaming cups.

'That was quick. Have you got one of those gas water heaters – a geezer?'

'No, why?'

'Roy makes me use ours for making drinks. He says it's cheaper than boiling a kettle.'

'Doesn't it taste a bit funny?'

'Does a bit.'

They both gave a little laugh at the silliness of the topic.

'There we go,' Mike passed her a cup, 'and here's the sugar if you want it.'

'Thanks, Mike, you're a real little housewife.'

'Uh, don't know about that. I could just about boil an egg. How is Roy's new job going?'

'OK, I think, he doesn't tell me much.'

She looked down at the floor as though she was ashamed of this fact.

114

'He'll be away a lot travelling and going into the head office in Reading.'

This seemed to cheer her up a little and a smile flickered across her face.

As they chatted about this and that, he watched the way her mouth moved and those little smiles that occasionally rippled across her lips. He liked Babs. He felt comfortable with her, despite the very unconventional way they had first got to know each other. And he preferred her to Julie, who was decidedly eccentric. Barbara looked vulnerable somehow, as though she was frightened about something. Mike found this rather appealing.

'Did you have a good night at Julie's the other night?'

He was taken back by this and suddenly felt a little bit vunerable. What had Julie been saying? What should he say? Should he be uncouth and say he had a great shag?

'Umm, fine thanks,' he replied, rather lamely.

'You can come and sit by me if you like,' Babs said coyly.

'OK.'

He crossed the small sitting room to join her on the sofa. She immediately put her hand on his thigh and Mike began to think this might not be a good idea in his own house, and the kids upstairs, but then again . . . He kissed her full on the lips. He hadn't kissed her before and it was very pleasant. Babs also seemed pleased.

'You're nice and gentle. You can show me what you did at Julie's if you like,' she murmured.

Mike inwardly groaned. Not all that rubbing again. He moved his hands under the full loose skirt. He easily lifted her knickers over her slender hips, down and off. Her legs parted willingly and fingers were soon probing the warm moistness, his thumb gently rubbing the important spot. Babs moaned with the prospect of impending pleasure, but Mike was already urgently unzipping his trousers and entering that wonderful warm, sensual place. All thoughts of whether it was a good idea or not had most decidedly left him.

'What was she doing here?' Jan demanded angrily. 'I wondered why Roy's car was behind me all the way home. I didn't know he was coming here though.'

'Roy just sort of left her here. Said he didn't have time or something to take her home.'

'Huh, or something. What's going on? You arranged this. You didn't use our bed did you?'

'No nothing, no of course not. Nothing happened,' he lied. Knowing she didn't believe him, he still added, 'We just talked that's all.'

'I don't want her here again. That Roy is a bloody menace. He's been hanging around me all night, leering, and carrying on about photos, asking me did I want to see them. There's something the matter with him. And you're involved with the creepy bugger.'

'I'm not involved with him, as you call it.'

'I'm not going to talk about it, I'm going to bed.'

Christ. Mike sat staring into space, shell-shocked by Jan's explosive reaction. I've never seen her so angry. And she swore. He had that horrible dragging sensation in his innards again. He felt so lonely, his brain numbed by the loss of more slender threads of friendship left between them, which was all they seemed to have left, and now that was lost. Why is she acting like this? She hadn't minded when he went to Roy's.

But then, perhaps it was a case of out of sight, out of mind. The only reason he could think of was that it involved their own home with the kids in it as well. Why had Roy brought Babs here? I had forgotten about the bloody photos. I wasn't there for that. Is he showing them around or what? I'll get them back somehow; at least there are no negatives. But why bring her here? He must have known what would happen. I don't like being pushed into things like this. I wish he hadn't brought her here. Oh sod her. Why should I worry about it? I enjoyed it. Still, what a bloody awful end to the day.

'Tell me what you and Mike did tonight, you slut. Go on, say it, everything. Shove the bottle in, harder. Do it, bitch.'

Unhappy, Jan was alone in bed and virtually hidden under the covers so as not to invite any of Mike's 'discussions'. She was unhappy about Barbara being in their own house with Mike, and miserable because the incident had again brought to the surface her perception of her own inadequacies. Her mood was not helped by the start of her monthly depression that she suffered from, even though the pill was supposed to help.

Jan believed the situation they had drifted into wouldn't have happened if she had been normal. 'I know that sex is really important to Mike and he fancies these other women because they're all slimmer than me and all appear to enjoy, it.' She felt helpless to change anything and wished it would all go away, be washed away, so they could start again. 'But then, I am what I am, and Mike is Mike, so nothing would change. Perhaps we should split up. But what about the kids? No, I don't want that. Maybe it will all end of its own accord. Maybe Babs and Jules, and whoever else he gets involved with, will all return to normal. Otherwise, what's the point of anyone getting married?' Julie hadn't said a word at rehearsals that night, nor had Jan, and Julie seemed to be her usual self and completely unaffected.

However, there was an overriding factor to Jan's ponderings. Despite her more public expressions of reservation, and denials of any interest in carnal matters, she was in reality as sexually curious as Mike and liked sex as much as Mike. Hers just took a slightly different form that's all. And she had already learned that other men excited her, even if they didn't satisfy her. So perhaps, when her depression lifted and her period was over, there might still be other adventures awaiting.

The next morning was cold and frosty, which matched the mood inside the house as well, but Mike had still given Jan a fleeting kiss upon the cheek. And after scraping the frost from the windscreen he set off to work.

'Yoh, Mike.' How ya doing?'

Crow was already in the locker room when Mike arrived.

'OK, Crow, me old mate. What's with the arm sling. What have you done?'

'Well, see I was painting the back of the house from on top of the wall, and I sort of forgot I was on the wall and I just stepped back to look at the good job I'd done and well, fell off.'

He gave a feeble laugh, but Mike laughed louder.

'Serves you right for not using a ladder, silly sod, you could have borrowed mine you know. Only had to ask.'

'Yeah, well, it's done now.'

'Should you be in work, Crow?'

'Yeah, it's not broken. Anyway, me and Sue had a really bad row, so I'd rather be here. It's going to be bloody odd, though,' he paused, taking a last drag of his cigarette and stubbing it out, 'having to come back in tonight for the night shift.'

'We'll get used to it.'

'Yeah, I suppose so. By the way, mate, I'd give Friday night a miss. Things are a bit bloody horrible at home. She's in a really bad mood.'

'Bad as that, eh?'

Mike could well imagine Susan in a temper. She was pretty noisy when things were going OK. When they weren't, well, it would be hell. He felt sorry for Crow. He was usually such an affable bloke.

118

'Yeah, bad bad.'

They both headed out into the lab in a dismal mood.

The morning passed by easily enough, as did the first and second night shift under the new scheme. And Mike was awoken by Jan at 2.00 on the Thursday afternoon.

He had to be up and about because Jan had yet more Christmas shopping to do 'the very last,' or so she said, and Mike had the piano arriving at three. He had told Crow on pain of death, or worse, not to tell Susan about the surprise, and he had then volunteered to help. But Mike had jokingly declined the offer, saying that a one-armed piano pusher wouldn't be much use. In any case, it would be up to the deliverymen to get into its temporary storage place in the disused shop.

Prompt at 3.00 p.m. the first stage of the secret mission took place without a hitch.

Mr Brown, the friendly shop owner, whose hairstyle and moustache made him a Hitler look-alike, turned up on the dot with key at the ready. Mind you, he didn't have far to travel because his functioning shop was only ten yards away. Even though the piano had been placed well away from the grimy, finger-stained windows of the old shop, Mike still covered it with pieces of dusty cardboard that were lying about the place – better safe than sorry. He was well pleased that all had gone so well and greeted Jan cheerfully when she arrived home.

'Blimey, is there anything left in the shops? Looks as though you've cleared them out.'

'You're in a good mood, so you can park the car around the corner for me. I'll get this lot upstairs before the kids see them.'

'Okey dokey,' Mike replied, taking the offered keys.

He parked the car in their usual spot off the main road and around the corner, next to the empty shop, well, not quite empty now. As he passed he looked in to see if anything could be seen of the piano by passers-by, but he had made a good job of it and it was well out of sight.

Back in the house, David and Mandy, having glimpsed the bag decorated with Christmas symbols, were running amok with anticipation. David, being the elder was more aware than his sister of the countdown to the big day, and would daily pass on the number of days to Mandy who would shriek with excitement. Mike and Jan thought the kids' enthusiasm was hectic but great fun, and the build-up to the great day was in some ways better than the day itself. It had been decided that this year Christmas Day dinner would be spent at Mike's mother's, and Boxing Day at Jan's. So for Jan, two days without cooking would be another Christmas present in itself. Nothing further had been mentioned about the Barbara business but the atmosphere was still cool, to say the least. But he would have to tell Janice that the visit to Crow's was off. He hesitated from saying anything in case the mention of marital conflict would start her off again about Babs, but it had to be done. Jan was in the kitchen putting away the shopping.

'Have you heard from Susan about going for a meal?' he asked tentatively.

'No. Should I? I don't usually, you see Crow all the time.' Her tone was cold.

'Well, they had had a bit of a row about something and Crow said would we mind if they call it off.'

'What's the row about, he must have told you?'

'No, just said things were bad at the minute.'

'Uh, I wonder what's he's been up to.'

She emphasised the 'he'.

Mike wanted to defend Crow by saying maybe it wasn't his fault, but thought better of it. He was just pleased that she hadn't used the information to rekindle their little argument of a few days ago.

'It doesn't matter. I will probably work that night anyway,' Jan said, finishing the unpacking and slumping down at the dining table and lighting up a cigarette.

'Do you want to try one of these Yankee fags, Phillip Morris? Crow put me on to them.'

Crow hadn't done any such thing; Mike just liked the look and feel of the paper packet, although the taste of the unfiltered toasted tobacco smoke was much nicer than his usual brand. He'd seen someone with them at work and liked the slick way you could shake one up out of the packet, as in the American films.

'They look a bit too strong for me.'

'Work at night?'

He just realised what Jan had said.

'They've asked me to work extra over Christmas, nights as well as lunchtimes. I said I would. The money will be good, and lots of tips. You don't mind, do you?'

'If you want to do it that's fine. I don't mind, but you don't have to, we manage OK,' Mike replied warmly, feeling great pride in Jan's dedication to the household budget.

However, the reason for Jan's decision was not as altruistic as it seemed.

The next day Mike took the kids to school and felt the need to see Babs and try to see if he could get hold of any photos of him and Babs and destroy them. He didn't actually hold out much hope of achieving this because he imagined Roy would have them well under his control. After dropping the children at the school gates, he set off on the short journey to Roy's place, hoping Barbara would be in.

Barbara was indeed at home and greeted him with quiet surprise and invited him in for a coffee.

'Roy's not here. He's been in Scotland, of all places.'

'Gets around a bit now doesn't he? Don't you mind?'

'Oh, I don't mind. He won't be back until tomorrow.'

121

Babs seemed pleased that his new job took him away from home.

'Right, do want that drink of coffee? I promise I won't make it from the geyser.'

They both laughed at the private joke. She appeared more relaxed than he usually saw her and looked less dishevelled, fresher somehow. He wasn't sure about mentioning the photos in case it stirred up memories she didn't want to recall.

'Um, do you remember the photos Roy took, you know, uh that night? Were there any of me, I mean us?'

His voice faded away at the expression he saw on her face. She was looking down at the floor, mumbling that she didn't remember, and he realised he had been right in his presumptions. He had wanted to ask her if she minded them being shown to everyone, if that was what he was doing, and exactly why she couldn't touch them, but she looked so downcast he changed the subject.

'All ready for Christmas, Babs?'

'Not really. I'm waiting for Roy to give me – I mean I'm waiting for Roy to be paid.'

'Oh right, expensive time of year. Nice coffee, want a ciggy? Oh no, you don't do you?'

'No, I don't smoke, Roy doesn't let me. He doesn't think it's nice.'

That's a laugh, Mike thought. Blimey, he allows her to have sex with other men, but makes a fuss about her having a ciggy. She was cheering up now and they chatted amiably about Christmas, the kids and other domestic topics, and he felt more comfortable and at ease than he had done for some time.

'It's time I made a move I suppose,' he said, making a move to get up.

He'd enjoyed the visit and Bab's company.

'Oh' she said, sounding disappointed at his departure.

She got up and crossed the room and quickly returned with a book, which she placed into his hands. Mike gave Barbara a puzzled look but she avoided his gaze.

'Have a read of this before you go, I think it's really sexy,' she said quietly.

He began reading and indeed found it quite arousing, and soon felt the need to touch himself surreptiously and adjust his underpants, using the book to cover his actions. He wondered what the hell this reading was all about and where Barbara had got to until he heard the now familiar gasping and moaning from the chair behind him. Turning slowly towards the sounds, he saw Babs, eyes closed, skirt drawn to her hips, knickers held aside, and her hand and fingers moving frantically. Briefly opening an eye, she murmured that Mike should do the same with himself because she wanted to watch him. He would have preferred to have real sex, but was so aroused at her suggestion and the highly erotic vision before him, that he readily complied.

Later he was on his way back home, without the photos but with another amazing, new and totally unexpected experience in his memory bank. This had been something very different. He had never seen a woman do that to herself, not even in the films at work. Mike, too, had surprised himself by doing something he normally only did in total privacy. He was now living in a different world, one in which sexual activity featured large and filled his thoughts for most of his waking hours. And his new philosophy was that sex is life, life is sex. Without sex there would be no life. He still wasn't getting enough of it – sex, that is. But what he was getting was massively exciting and Mike was, nevertheless exhilarated. Christmas and a healthy pay raise on its way, he and Jan still together, albeit sexless, the kids healthy, life was good.

What a morning – bloody fantastic!

Reaching home, Jan was taking the opportunity of being without the children, to pack presents.

'You were a long time.'

'Yeah, bumped into someone from work,' Mike lied.

'They're all done,' she said, giving a big sigh of relief, and packing the scattered bits of Christmas paper, tinsel and labels back into her 'Christmas box'.

'What day shall we take the kiddies into town?'

'Bit early yet. Let's leave it until nearer Christmas Eve, it's more exciting then.'

'OK, it will be busier though.'

'Doesn't matter. We'll cope, we usually do.'

'What do you want for lunch? I've got to go to work soon. I'll be back to feed you all, and then I'm back in work but I'm not sure what time we finish. Is that OK?'

'Yep, I'll cope.'

13

'Two pints, over here, Darling.'

'Patience, patience, I've only got one pair of hands,' Jan responded with a smile.

'And what a pair,' his eyes indicating that it wasn't her hands he was referring to.

Jan, with her now well-established barmaid confidence and experience knew what he really meant. She liked it when it was busy and the atmosphere full of cigarette smoke and disjointed bits of conversation, plus the occasional girlish shriek – from the women. Observing all the movements and activities from behind the bar, the whole ambiance of the place in fact, was like a stage-setting, just like one of the plays she had often acted in and not real at all. Janice, too, had an air of indifference and unreality about her and believed if she wanted to she could just walk off stage whenever she pleased. This was certainly better than sitting at home watching the telly or sewing – and was one of the reasons she had agreed to the extra hours, and, of course, the other was that there were new people to meet . . .

The management, with Christmas decorations to maximise the *bonhomie* and increase drink consumption, had already bedecked the place. And tonight the policy was working well because the place was full. Jan found that it was an entirely different crowd in the evenings, although one or two lunchtime regulars were also present. Jan was glad of this because it gave the job a sense of continuity and she appreciated the friendly faces, not that she had to cope on her own, as there was another barmaid, Shirley, with her. But Jan hadn't met her before and had to get to know her. Tony hadn't been in at all that day, for which she was grateful. It left her free to concentrate on the increased workload. He was still pursuing her and she was trying to cool his interest, but this was proving a bit difficult, so his every absence was, to Jan, a blessing.

As it happened, there were number of off-duty policemen amongst the throng and it was one of these happy bobbies who was propping up the bar.

'I know where you live, gorgeous,' he said, taking a swig of his pint.

'Oh yes, and how do you know that then?'

Jan recognised the fresh faced, fair-haired man who looked younger than her, from the previous lunchtime, although he wasn't a regular. Indeed, she had found him very attractive and wasn't unhappy at seeing him again.

''Cos I'm a policmen. And I know where your husband works.'

'That will be three and sixpence, please,' Jan said, as she continued serving other people arriving at the bar from stage left, right and centre. And she'd quickly learnt how to serve and still keep a conversation going with men who propped up the bar.

'And how do you know that?' Jan continued.

'I followed you.'

'Oh, yes, did you now. And should you be doing that? following innocent people around?' Jan retorted cheerfully, not really believing a word his beer was saying to her.

'Only if they're as lovely as you, Janice.'

'Oh, yes, so you know my name then. And what's yours.' Jan laughed, and continued to serve another customer.

'Alan. But you can call me Al and another pint for me, please.'

'I think you've had enough,' said Jan but continued to pull his drink and place it in front of him.

The evening moved on and last orders, time arrived, which was greeted by the usual groans of disappointment from the patrons, and a dash to the bar for that last drink for the road.

'Do want a lift home, Janice?' Alan asked, with what Jan considered a pleasing impish smile.

'I've got a car, thanks. In any case, I think you're younger than me. I should be seeing you home,' Jan joked.

'OK, you follow me in your car and I'll give you a nice cup of coffee for your trouble. OK?'

He staggered slightly as he headed to the exit and out into the night.

'OK. I'll see you outside. I'll be about hour. Got to clear up first.'

Jan couldn't believe what she had just said. What am I doing, he can't be more than 19 or 20 years old. Not a big difference I know, but he seems so young, and well, innocent. And he has nice hands, like Mike. She wished she hadn't made that mental comparison.

When Jan eventually finished clearing the glasses and went outside it was raining and cold with it. Jan thought Alan must have been freezing; his car was too old to have a heater. Still the booze would keep him warm. Perhaps he'd gone home and that would be that. But he was still waiting, sitting in his car. She half-hoped he wouldn't have been there, and then the smattering of guilt she had about her behaviour wouldn't bother her. However, the excitement at the sense of freedom she was experiencing was compensating for that.

Mike looked at the clock on the bedside table. 11.30 p.m., where the hell was she? He had gone to bed at 11.00, which was late for him after a night shift, but couldn't sleep until he knew Jan was home. The problem was he didn't know what time she was supposed to finish. Not being a pub goer he had no idea of the times involved. He was becoming more concerned as the minutes went by. He got up, went downstairs and lit up a cigarette, and then felt annoyed that he would now have to clean his teeth again after the fag. He couldn't sleep with a smoky mouth, uck.

She followed Alan's car to a street off the town centre where Alan had a small second-floor flat. Once inside Jan could see he was a little worse for wear and set about making the coffee herself.

'Here, drink this, you silly boy, I told you not to drink so much.'

She sounded almost motherly but inside she felt in total control of the situation – and of Alan.

The room was set out as a bed-sit with a separate tiny kitchen and bathroom and Alan was half-lying on the single bed. She sat beside him sipping her coffee, which she really didn't want but it gave her time to take stock of Alan and the surroundings.

She noticed the time on the clock on the bedside cupboard but it didn't really register how late for her, and Mike, it was. But to her she was still an actor in a play that hadn't yet finished, and this particular scene of being in a strange room, with a strange man, was proving to be rather arousing. Her body was responding to her mental antici-pation and she was waiting for Alan to make a move. However, away from the pub he seemed a little bit lost as to what to do next and the drink was having a bad effect on his body.

11.45 p.m. Where is she? Mike was on his second ciggy and he was now very agited. Was she with someone? This was, of course, a possiblity. After all, she got to know Tony from the hotel, and look what happened there. Or was

128

there something wrong at the hotel? His brain was racing with a mixture of concern, jealously and anger, angry with Jan for not telling him she was going to be so late and jealous at the possibility of her being with someone he didn't know, or that she might be enjoying herself too much, or perhaps discussing him. He wanted to know what was going on. His stomach was churning with the nervous tension. He hated not knowing. If they had properly discussed this sort of behaviour it might not seem so bad. But they hadn't talked about anything for ages and ages. He lit yet another cigarette and stared out of the window at the deserted, wet and silent street.

Alan by now had brightened a little and had made a couple of attempts at kissing Jan and fondling her breasts through her clothes. But it was beginning to look as though he wouldn't be attempting much else, for a while at least.

'Did you really follow me?' Jan asked quizzically.

'Yeah.'

'Why follow me, an old married woman, and with two kids?'

'I fancied you. You're a good looker, and you're not old, and, well, you're more sensible than well, you know, than girls.'

Jan didn't know quite how to take that, but thought it was a compliment. Not that she was much concerned with the content of what he said. After all, they were only lines in a play. And besides, she was beginning to think he was a virgin and had chosen her as the least threatening female to try his luck with. This thought gave Jan's confidence and arousal levels a big kick, because if her theory was correct then she was now definitely in control. Jan liked that idea very much. If he knew nothing about women, then he couldn't judge her.

Mike sat in the chair drinking coffee, not the best drink at night, but he was smoking so much in an attempt to ease his agitation that his throat was dry, and he found the coffee soothing. This was not a situation he wanted to be in. She must be with someone. But why at this time of night and who was he? It must be a he. Could it be Tony? He thought not, though he could be wrong. This not knowing what was going on made him feel immensely insecure and vunerable. It was not so much about the sex, although if she was now that interested in sex why not with him, her husband? He had been looking for sex. What was Jan looking for? His heart was racing and his head ached with endless scenarios tumbling about his brain. In his almost demented frame of mind he felt as though the essence of who and what he was, his whole world was being threatened in some way. It was irrational. This was not how he wanted it to be.

The clock read 12.30 a.m. Mike decided to go back to bed. Surely she would be back soon.

Janice closed the car door as quietly as possible. It was late, the rain had stopped, and most houses were in darkness and all was very quiet, and she felt guilty about making a noise. She grimaced as the engine roared to life, making the careful shutting of the door seem grossly superfluous.

It was now her turn to feel pleased with herself. Alan had been, in Jan's eyes, unusually sweet and innocent and had admitted he hadn't ever been with a woman.

He had been desperate to change all that with someone whom he felt safe with, as indeed most people do. But for a young man to admit such a state of affairs in the middle of an alleged sexual revolution, or at any time really, Jan thought was very brave, and exceptional. Mind you, his fragile condition might have helped a little to break any reticence he might have had. To Jan's surprise, he really was a policeman, but only a cadet and from Gloucester, a long way from Baray. But it seemed it was policy to move them from their hometown whenever possible in case familiarity with the local populace led to favouritism. It also transpired that some of his fellow cadets had quickly realised that he was a virgin and made his life hell.

Janice had found it extremely exciting showing Alan what was what, and was thrilled by his tentative boyish, touching and exploration and amazed Alan and herself by stimulating herself in front of him, something she hadn't ever done with Mike. But, of course, this wasn't for real, only a make believe drama.

She still felt strangely distant from her normal world and it was not unpleasant, rather like being single again and without domestic and wifely duties. And she had experienced a sense of being on equal sexual terms with Alan. He a virgin, she, in her opinion a dysfunctional woman unable to get sexual contentment from Mike, and so far with any man, from 'normal' sex. In her mind Mike had in a way taken control of her sex life and wanted to make it his own. But she believed that all men were 'normal' and knew instinctively what to do sexually. And women, if they loved the man, would, should, respond. And basically that was that. It was only a freak like her, with her secret 'sin' that was the exception to the rule.

Reaching home, she crept up the stairs undressing as she went and slid into bed next to Mike, who sighed a sigh of relief, said nothing, and both were soon asleep.

14

The trouble with trouble is, that once it begins it doesn't know when to stop – as his grandmother used to say.

'David, come on, I've got shopping to do,' Jan shouted up the stairs.

Mandy was already down and almost dressed. Mike, exhausted by his worrisome night waiting for Jan to return, was still in bed but awake and listening to the household activity, and thinking, again. He was still very peeved with Jan for staying out so late without telling him what she was doing. Yes, OK, he had been to Babs the other morning, but that was different. He wasn't out half the night with Gods knows who, or where. This is not how it should work. Why couldn't they talk about what they were doing?

He was beginning to think that Roy had a lot to answer for. He started all this, didn't he? But then he had gone along with this wife-swapping lark readily enough and still found the whole idea, and Bab's amenable willingness, very compelling. However, Mike's life with Jan wasn't improving. If anything they were further apart than ever.

'Here, sweetheart, let me help you. Put your arm in this way. Now the other one. There, all ready now, eat your breakfast, there's a good girl. David, I won't tell you again,' Jan shouted.

There were mumblings and rumblings from somewhere upstairs, then much louder thumps and bumps and a yell.

132

Crying followed and yowls of pain. Mike's voice then joined the other noises on the stairway.

'What the hell is going on, what happened, son?'

'I fell down the stairs and my arm is hurting,' David sobbed, clutching his left arm to his chest.

Jan and Mike helped David to his feet and tried to make him comfortable in a chair but at every move David yelled with pain.

'He must have broken it, I'll get dressed and we'll get him to the hospital,' Mike said, running up the stairs to get ready.

'God, I could have done with out this today and I've got so much to do. I'll go and see if Rita can look after Mandy for a couple of hours.'

'OK', Mike shouted down to Jan. 'I won't be long.'

Mandy sat chomping on her breakfast, one arm propping up her head, the other shovelling food in a totally unconcerned manner, unusual for her, as normally a feather blowing in the breeze would worry her. The look on her little face was almost distainful, as though to say 'typical, silly boy'.

'I don't want to go to hospital,' whined David.

'You should have thought of that before. What were you doing anyway, all that banging about upstairs?'

'I was being superman.'

David was always trying to emulate his latest hero.

'Well, darling, unfortunately you're not and now you've hurt yourself.'

At this he started to cry again.

'It will be all right. Don't cry, and be a brave boy.'

Jan bent and kissed him.

Mike returned dressed and with car keys in hand.

'Right, I better get to Rita's in case she's going out. You try and get a coat on him. It's cold outside.'

Mike couldn't get a coat on the little lad so he draped it

over David's shoulders, but even this was difficult. Janice returned, grabbed Mandy and dashed back to Rita's.

Soon they were in the car and heading for the small local hospital.

They were at their best in a crisis and they still could work as a team. Whether it was a childhood illness, or Mike hitting a nail through the water pipe when he replaced some floorboards, their differences and problematic sex life were forgotten. All their thoughts concentrated upon solving the issue.

The nurse at local hospital was sullen and efficient, and unhelpful.

'We can't do anything here I'm afraid. You'll have to go to the general hospital in Aberdod. He might need anaesthetic so it can be set. Can't do that here. Sorry.'

Mike and Jan were not amused at this prospect, but drove off as fast as the pre-Christmas Saturday shopping traffic to Aberdod would allow.

'If we had a phone we could have saved time by ringing the hospital first. We could have gone straight to Aberdod – we'd be there by now. We might have missed the traffic.'

'I expect it would have been useful, but I have been busy, you know, what with Christmas and the rehearsals. I haven't exactly been idle. Anyway, why have I got to do it? You could sort it out when you're not in work. I've got enough to do seeing to the kids and one thing and another.'

'OK, OK, no need to bite my head off.'

Jan hadn't done anything about getting a phone. It had somehow slipped her mind. After all, she had been rather busy in other directions. She was irritable too. But in a resentful sort of way. She wanted more time to herself to explore what had become a separate way of living. Her adventures were less about sex and more about personal freedom. She had come to the conclusion that marriage was a much bigger life change for women than for men,

134

and was beginning to wish that she wasn't married, and realised that she had missed out on a lot of life. Men didn't have the children, and went off to work much as they did when they were at home with mummy. Clothes were washed and husbands fed, very little changed for them. And then they expected sex on tap, or at least that's how the world was looking to Jan on this troublesome day.

She was dreading him coming home for the weekend. She had become relaxed without him and even the kids had been happier, laughing and playing unconcernedly.

He would he home soon.

'Has he had anything to eat this morning?' the nurse asked in a voice as crisp as her uniform looked.

'No, nothing,' Mike and Jan said in unison.

'Right, you'll have to leave him with us. It's a bad break. He will have to go to theatre to have it set. It will be best if you go home and come back this afternoon. It might be best if you give us a ring first.'

Mike and Jan looked at each other utterly crestfallen. Leaving their beloved son, alone, didn't appeal to them at all. Jan's eyes began to fill with tears as she kissed David goodbye and Mike reassured him all would be well and they would see him soon. David, in the contrary way children have, seemed surprisingly unconcerned and was busy examining all the bits of medical gear around the casualty bed he was sitting on.

The nurse pushed them out of the cubicle and into the corridor. Mike's eyes were also tearful as he put his arm around Janice's shoulders and they walked slowly out of the hospital.

The drive home was quiet. Neither said a lot. Mike gently mentioned that he would sort the phone business himself but Jan, feeling a little more mellow, agreed that she would make serious enquiries and get the ball rolling. It was too late for Mike to contact work to get the afternoon off and decided that he would go in anyway. Jan would have to ring the works after contacting the hospital. The plan was he would then come home, pick Jan up and they could go to the hospital together. Jan's shopping would now have to wait until Monday. If she was desperate for anything she could always pop into Mr 'Hitler' Brown's corner shop and pick up a few things.

And, ironically, on the way home they had to stop to use a public phone box again for Janice to make a call to Julie. She had arranged for her to pick her up at three to go to rehearsals, but wouldn't bother now and would stay at home.

By the time they did get home it was nigh on time for Mike to go to work and the morning had shown Mike just how easily plans could be thwarted. While Jan was out doing the weekly shop around town he had intended to do some shopping himself for some little presents for Jan. She had to have something to open upstairs with the children, because usually the kids came into their room at the crack of dawn to unpack their presents and Jan and Mike opened theirs at the same time, so she would be a little bit perplexed if she didn't have anything. He would have had to be careful though, making sure he didn't meet Jan as she went from shop to shop, up and down the town, buying the foodstuffs. Jan had a system. She would start from the town hall and library at the centre of town. Then shop down one side of Olton Road, the High Street, and back up the other, sometimes stopping half way for coffee and a cigarette, depending whether or not she had Mandy in tow. If Mike did see her, once he knew in which direction she was going, he could avoid her. Still all this was rather academic for today. The factory beckoned.

*

Barbara was at the kitchen sink washing dishes when Roy got home that afternoon. She turned to greet him as cheerfully as she could pretend, but he roughly turned her around and pushed her against the sink.

'Bend over, you sodding bitch.'

As he spoke he hoisted up her skirt and pulled her knickers aside.

'Who's been shagging you while I've been away, you slut?'

'No one. Honest, Roy, no one.'

'Shut up, you liar. Bend over, you tart, you're going to get it now. Like a dog.'

'Please, no, Roy, not there. It hurts too much, please don't do it.'

'Shut your mouth, unless you want a slap – bend over – you slut.'

'Oh God, no, Roy, please don't hurt me.'

'He did a better job then me, really broke it, eh?' Crow said.

'Yeah, well, he's cleverer than you, and better looking. Follows his dad.'

'Ha, bloody ha ha,' Crow laughed, greatly enjoying the banter – he needed cheering up too.

Mike was grateful for the light relief he was experiencing with Crow and was glad he had come into work. Their lighthearted repartee had put his concern for his little son into a less emotional perspective. Not only that, it was pay day.

It was the first pay day under the new management and for the last time the payslips were to be collected from the old pay office where they used to pick up their weekly pay packets of cash. Now all the pay had to go into a bank once a month, and most staff already missed the satisfaction of getting real money in their hand. All they would receive today would be a bit of paper telling them how much had gone into their accounts.

Choosing a bank had been an interesting occasion and

something that Mike never thought he would be doing. As far as he knew, his works were the first business in the town to make their workers, chequebook holders. Mike saw it as a definite move up the social ladder. The only other people he knew of with a chequebook were either posh, rich, or both. All the local banks had set up tables in the cavernous site canteen. Well, in fact there were two, one for workers in dirty clothes, and the other called the staff canteen, for clean workers, and each could seat about 300 people. Mike was eligible for the 'clean' end but very rarely ate there. No real money changed hands because payment was by tokens only, plastic ones naturally, but it was a pain remembering to buy them before they were needed. Mind you Mike always had a few with him for paying the tea trolley lady who came around the lab during the day dispensing teas and buns. Naturally, the banks choose the staff canteen for the exercise, where they handed out leaflets, it was then just a matter of choosing the one you fancied. Mike had gone for Williams and Glyn, a bank new to the town and affiliated to the Royal Bank of Scotland, maybe a strange choice for a Welshman but he liked the down-to-earth attitude of the staff and certainly didn't like the attitude of the Barclay people – too snooty for him.

The new management had promised the new pay rates would be for the full month even though the changes had only been in place for a couple of weeks. And Mike hoped that wasn't about to change. There was a quiet air of excitement in the lab as people waited to see what monies they were going to get.

'Coming for a cuppa, Mike?'

'Might as well, not much on today, is there?'

'It's the run up to Christmas 'innit? Who wants tons of smelly resin hanging about at Christmas?'

'We do, if we want to keep our jobs.'

138

'Yeah, yeah – Mr Bloody Serious. Get the kettle on, and cheer up, it's payday.'

'Want a ciggy?' Mike asked.

'Are you still on those Yankee fags?'

'Yep.'

'Then no, they're bloody awful.'

'No taste, no style, that's your trouble, mate,' Mike said as he puffed with exaggerated pleasure.

'Hey, Crow, how are things with you and Sue these days?'

'Not much better, worse if anything.'

'Sorry about that, mate.'

Crow just shrugged his shoulders and set about making the drinks.

Later, with coffee and Mars bars consumed, they ate a lot of these, it was time for the last trek to the pay office. Not that they had far to go, as it was only about 50 yards away from the lab.

'Let's go and see what we've got, matey.' Might be enough for you to get a better car, Crow.'

'Fat chance.'

There was a short straggly queue shuffling past the little pay office window. The pay Clerk, nicknamed 'Fag Ash Dave' always had a fag in his mouth and had a wonderful technique of blowing the ash from the cigarette without removing it from his mouth. When he did so clouds of ash would go in all directions. His action fascinated many, and people would watch for the white stick of ash to grow, and then duck when a blowing was due. Mike wondered if he was related to the caretaker of the community hall who had a similar technique.

It was Mike's turn to receive the small brown envelope.

'Good times are here again,' Mike said cheerfully, 'thanks Dave.'

'Huh, make the most of it, mate.'

His cigarette, stuck on to his lower lip jiggled about as he spoke. Mike laughed at Dave's miserable demeanour.

'And a Merry Christmas to you too.'

Mike and Crow walked back to the lab, eagerly tearing open the packets and reading the details as they went.

'Bloody hell, Crow, we are now thousandaires. With the shift allowance it's one thousand two hundred a year. That's twenty-three pounds a week. Bloody hell, that's fantastic.'

Crow was equally shocked and pleased.

'Might change the car after all. I could afford to buy it on the old hire purchase now.'

'Bloody great, eh, Crow? Do you know, I don't think that Fag Ash ever smiles? You'd think even he would be happy today, wouldn't you?'

'He's always a miserable bugger, who cares – over twenty quid a week, bloody great. I'm so chuffed I could even smoke one of your horrible Yankee fags now, to celebrate.'

At about 4.00 p.m. Mike received the call from Janice to say that David was ready to come home and he set off home. He was excited about telling Jan the long-awaited news about the pay rise. That should cheer her up a little. However, on the downside, Mike's analytical and cautious mind couldn't avoid considering why Fag Ash had made the comments he had. Was there something nasty lurking in the pay office?

'That Roy has been here and left you some photos, said you asked Barbara for them the other day. When did you call there? You didn't say.'

Jan was in ice mode, and her announcement was like a slap on the face. Jan had hardly given him time to come through the front door before she began her lecture and Mike hadn't had a chance to mention the pay rise and he was totally taken by surprise at the news. Babs must have told Roy. Why had she done that? He had the impression that she didn't want to talk about the photos. He wasn't pleased with Roy either. Why involve Jan? Was he trying to cause trouble? He must be very thick skinned if he couldn't recognise Jan's dislike of him.

'I um, bumped into her, somewhere, I eh can't remember where now.'

Why am I lying? What's the point of it? He tried changing the subject but Jan hadn't quite finished.

'Is that what you like now is it – having your picture taken doing you know what? You're as sick as he is.'

'You've seen them?'

'Of course I've seen them. He made sure of that, and he wanted to know why I wouldn't get involved in his little games. He's not all there, in his head. He gives me the creeps.'

'Bloody hell, that's a bit much, and I'm not sick as you call it, it's what he wanted to do – not me. I didn't know he was taking pictures of me. And anyway, if you were a bit more interested in sex I wouldn't be involved in the first place.'

'That's right, blame me for everything, I wondered when you'd bring all that up again, and it's no excuse anyway and we're not starting all that now, we've got to get to Aberdod. Oh, one last thing, he said for you to call at his place anytime. I don't know what you see in him, he's not your type.'

No, but his wife is, Mike thought, and I think that remark means, see Babs anytime, and I intend to. He certainly is an odd one; I wouldn't like Jan seeing other men all the time. Christ, what a bastard though, showing Jan those pictures.

God, my grandmother has a lot to answer for, she used to say trouble came in threes.

Let's hope she's wrong – for once.

'We can't avoid him anyway because we're bound to see him at the am dram.'

'And that's another thing, I don't know why he's there, he's useless. He can't sing – or act.'

'I wouldn't know about that.'

'Yes, well, come on, we must go. I'll collect Mandy from Rita's when we get back.'

Jan's tone said, 'that's all for now' and the tirade ended.

Jan's anger about Roy was real enough. She didn't like him and didn't want him in their house. And she would be happier if Mike didn't have any more to do with him. But she had encouraged Mike to go to Roy's and get involved in the first place, although she realised he probably would have gone anyway. However, she was once again angry with herself, or perhaps more accurately with her reactions to the photographs, and for taking it out on Mike. After Roy had gone she had sat at the dining table looking though them again. The novelty of seeing such images, for the first time, of real people she knew having real sex had been highly arousing, rather as she imagined it would be watching them in the flesh, as it were. So powerful had been her response that despite all the other problems of the day, she could not resist, there and then, to satisfy her excitement.

On the drive to the hospital, Mike at last had a chance to show Janice the payslip, which pleased her as much as it had him. She had calmed down since their earlier confrontation and their conversation took on a slightly friendlier note.

'It's a pity we can't save some of it. You know, towards another house or something.'

'Nice idea, but the kids cost more and more as they grow up. Perhaps we should take out an endowment policy or something like that for the future,' Jan suggested.

'That's a good idea. Why don't you have a word with Bill next time you go to rehearsals? Ask him to call. Might as well give him the business, he's a nice bloke.'

David was surprisingly frisky when they picked him up

from the hospital and the only thing he was concerned about was food as the poor lad hadn't had anything to eat all day, and, of course showing off his plaster cast and arm sling to anyone with the mildest degree of sympathy.

'I'll tell you what, why don't we stop and buy fish and chips or something on the way back and take them home? It will save you cooking.'

'That would be nice,' Jan said, giving a rare smile.

'Can I have chicken and chips, Dad?'

'Of course you can, son. It's a celebration.'

'Dad, what's a celebration?'

'That's my boy. It's good to have you back, sunshine.'

Mike chuckled, as he playfully ruffled David's hair.

What was left of the weekend passed uneventfully and Mike's shift cycle ended after nights at 8.00 a.m. the following Thursday. He now had four days off and he intended calling on Babs, and he had been wondering why they hadn't heard from Julie. He wouldn't mind trying a rerun with Julie sometime. She might teach him something else that was new. He'd asked Jan if it wasn't time that they invited them to their place. She hadn't seemed too keen on the idea, and said that they didn't have room to put them up for the night, and to wait to be invited again. Mike thought not returning the evening was a bit impolite, but went along with Jan's comments.

Of course, in reality Jan didn't want to bother with Tony again after her disappointing time with him, and she had been putting Julie off by saying they were too busy with Christmas. She wouldn't mind seeing Alan again, with whom she could relax and pretend to be someone else, and hoped he would want to see her again. The fact that neither Mike nor any of her friends had ever met him had added to the play-acting fantasy, an element in her life which she didn't want to lose – for now.

15

There were now only 12 days to Christmas and there were already many Christmas trees on display in front windows along the streets. And whenever they were all in the car, as a family, driving here and there, they would play count the Christmas tree game, at which Mandy usually became very frustrated because she really couldn't count very well. It was all great fun and Mike wished it would be the same this year, despite the coolness between him and Jan.

The town square too would soon have a huge tree and evening carol singing sessions, and the children's visit to Santa's grotto was imminent. Mike had enjoyed this a lot when he was a child and loved to see his own kids, faces full of awe and amazement. Hopefully they would have a great time, especially now that they had some extra spending money. They usually only visited one Santa, the one that Mike and Jan thought looked the most 'realistic', but at least two of the best grottoes in the biggest shops in Aberdod, and everyone would be exhausted by the end of the day.

Mike still had to shop for some little gifts for Janice, and even though she continued her indifferent attitude towards him, perhaps Christmas would be a good time to try and make a fresh start. He hoped the special gift would do the trick. But he wasn't holding his breath. Indeed, during those treasured silent moments before sleep he had spent time sort of updating his mind, and trying to evaluate what had, and was, happening to them. At face value no one could tell that anything had changed. And when at his or her parents, or with friends, they would appear as though everything was normal. It was a strange situation.

In some ways nothing had changed and there were still the common interests of the children, the house, the household budget, and a million everyday actions, all unchanged. It was sex, this one extraordinary facet of their lives, that was the important oddity. In a strange way he felt their escapades were strengthening, and yet at the same time, undermining their marriage. But which was gaining, the weakening or the strengthening? At the moment he thought it was weakening. But then events in their lives had always waxed and waned, like the moon, just as the pattern of life for most people varies, some days good, some not so good.

If only they could talk quietly and rationally to each other, discuss in some depth about where they were going with their lives. Perhaps then Mike would discover who Jan was with the other night. If he could see the bloke, perhaps talk to him, he then might not consider him a threat. For instance, he wasn't worried about Tony. He had seen him in his home world and that made a difference. And certainly not Crow. Not that anything had happened on that front. But whenever it came into his mind, the not knowing, it still gnawed holes in his gut and he tried to shut it out. Jan's silence seemed ominous.

Despite these dark and pessimistic before-sleep ideas, in daylight hours he was a little more cheerful and confident and wanted to visit Babs – she was the only woman available to him, and he wanted real sex instead of his own secret self-ministrations.

Mike was becoming used to ringing the doorbell at Roy's,

and once again he was lucky, as he expected to be. Roy was at work.

'Just passing, thought I'd call in. Where is he this week, Babs?' Mike said jauntily, his manner belying the real, lustful purpose of his visit.

'Cornwall,' Babs replied, shutting the door behind them.

'Blimey, he does a lot of driving.'

'He says he likes it.'

He did. Roy had very quickly found that a smart company car had a good effect on impressionable young women he met. Plus, of course, the money he was spending on them.

'Expect you want coffee, Mike. With real hot water.'

They both giggled at their ongoing standing joke.

'When the door rang I thought you were the milkman.'

'The milkman?'

'Roy,' she hesitated and seemed embarrassed, 'forgot to leave me any money to pay him.'

'Oh, right, I thought you looked worried when you opened the door. Not to worry. If he calls I've got a few bob with me, you can owe me.'

'That's nice of you but I don't think he'll call now, it's getting too late for him.'

'That's OK, if you're sure.'

The coffee made, they sat opposite each other, each of them lost in the huge acreage of the two luxurious sofas.

'Christmas soon, Babs. I see you've got some decorations.'

'The girls were nagging the life out of me so I put a few things up, we haven't got many,' she said wistfully.

'We must get ours sorted too. The kids are driving me mad about it as well.'

'Where are your two today?'

'At the nursery school, gives me a bit of peace for a few hours.'

She gave him one of her smiles, her brown eyes shining.

Mike thought she looked very desirable and went and sat close beside her.

'By the way, I got the photos, from Roy. He brought them over the other day.'

'I know.'

She hung her head again. Surely the photos shouldn't bother her that much. It was ages ago anyhow. Perhaps there was another reason.

'Did you tell him I called? They weren't that important,' Mike lied, but was curious as to why Roy had made the effort to call.

'I had to tell him,' she said, quietly staring into her coffee.

Tears began to fall; she struggled to hold back her sobs. Mike put his arm around her and felt a surge of sympathetic affection, and passion, and found her vulnerability strangely arousing.

'Don't cry, Babs. What's the matter? Here have this.'

Mike handed her his handkerchief.

'Nothing really. I'm just a bit down that's all. You're so nice to me.'

She turned to him, gave him a quick kiss on the mouth.

'Will you come to bed with me, now, and love and cuddle me?'

Mike was taken aback, and the word 'love' caused him a very temporary panic. Surely that's not an expression wife-swappers use. He very rapidly concluded that perhaps to Babs it was a pseudonym for sex, and quickly responded to the idea.

'Of course, if that's what you want.'

It seemed a bit odd to Mike that as a cure for her sadness he was going to get joy. They got up and Babs led them to the bedroom.

Later, as they lay naked and entwined, warm skin to skin,

something he hadn't done with other women, only Jan, and in Mike's mind it made the occasion more intimate, perhaps even loving. This was different from the times with Susan and Julie.

Babs hadn't been concerned with her satisfaction. She wanted, needed, gentle affection. It was something he had in abundance to give. He had taken time, moved slowly, gently, and bestowed kisses on breasts, face and shoulders. She had too moved with gentle rhythm, returning kisses, quietly purring and smiling with happiness.

In that time after passion has died, words are often spoken that are rarely said at other times.

'I like you a lot, Mike. Do you like me?' she said softly, lightly running her fingers over his chest. 'I wish I lived with you,' she added.

Mike didn't know what to say. He was sated, relaxed, though feeling that he was now really betraying his commitment to Jan. This encounter has been more emotional than any of the others and it had caught him by surprise. He wanted to say something nice and kind, something tender, but held back. Quickies, with most of your clothes on, or kinky photo sessions, were not like times such as these. Luckily for him, before he had formulated a reply, Babs broke the silence.

'I didn't want to do all that photographing business, and all those other men. Roy wants me to do it. We were married in church in the eyes of God and I shouldn't be doing things like this, it's not right.'

She looked sad again. She and Roy had never indulged in any sexual hanky panky before they were married. Bab's parents were quite religious and as she had been an only child she was totally influenced by her parents' religious fervour. She and her parents had thought Roy to be a very nice boy but Babs would not allow any ungodly behaviour

148

like touching any naughty bits. Mike was taken aback by her remarks. All those men? Bloody hell, just how many had there been? Was she religious? Or joking or a little disturbed? Maybe both. It just didn't sound quite right; he just hoped she wouldn't start crying again.

The front door bell rang and suddenly the surreal, intimate spell was broken and Babs leapt out of bed.

'It could just be the milkman, but it could be my mother.' She frantically pulled on a jumper and skirt. 'I'd forgotten she said she might call.'

'Oh bloody hell, your mother? Where are my trousers? Look, here's a quid in case it's the milkman. Don't argue, take it. I'll get dressed and wait in the living room, OK?'

Babs nodded in agreement and rushed towards the stairs.

Babs had given him much food for thought. Just where is the dividing line between love and just sex? Mike decided there must be one but knowing where to draw it was the difficulty. He decided that for him there must be some degree of affection and respect for the woman. He already had plenty of that for Jan. It was the sex part that was missing. He didn't think that he would want to exchange what he already had, simply for sexual satisfaction. Although it was easy for him to be thinking this way now, when his appetite for sex had just been slaked, but what was he to do when his hunger returned?

He really liked Babs. She was so very relaxed and frank about what she liked in bed and seemed to need as much as he did. And to be honest, he had missed expressing and experiencing warm, protective thoughts towards a woman, and he had enjoyed this part of the event as much as the sex. Should he contemplate the idea of divorce or separation? He wouldn't just be giving up a person but a whole way of life. He knew Jan and she knew him, well, as much as any individual can know another.

Because in truth we are all alone within ourselves, but the illusion of knowing, the tolerance of differences, is what we all search for, and cherish.

Worryingly, he didn't know what Jan was thinking about their life together.

He was back in the house by lunchtime and Jan had already left for the hotel. Shirley, the other barmaid, had given her a lift so that Mike could have the car to pick up the kids from school. He had meant to get the gifts for Jan during the morning but had been somewhat sidetracked by the visit to Barbara's – and the arrival of her mother. So he would get himself something to eat and get his shopping done that afternoon, and include a visit to the library, pick up some books – great. He was actually looking forward to his leisurely stroll around town amongst the Christmas tinsel, browsing the shops for gifts. It might also take his mind off Barbara.

Friday afternoon and Roy was drinking coffee in a road-side cafe taking a break from the long drive back to Wales. He was very pleased with himself. During his working visits to doctors and hospitals, he had met a couple of suitably gullible and compliant young women – just the sort he liked, and with a bit of luck his future visits would include some female company. For the time being he would have to put up with stupid Barbara and his miserable kids.

His parents were out at the pub and he was doing what his parents had told him to do, although this time was a little different. He was, yet again, keeping an eye on his sister who hadn't ever been 'very well in the head'.

Roy was looking at her through the partly opened bedroom door. The room was small and decorated with infantile patterned wall-paper, and equally naive tiny-tot dolls and toys littered the floor. His sister was naked, sitting on her bed. The expression on her

150

fresh 15-year-old face was one of utter fascination and amazment, as though this was the first time she had discovered the miraculous changes, when, in fact, it occupied much of her time. She was examining, once again, the triangle of hair between her legs, gently pulling a strand or two testing how long they might be.

Continuing his furtive watching, Roy too was fascinated, and immensely aroused. At 16 he had never seen a naked female. He shifted his position slightly and she looked up noticing him for the first time, but was totally unabashed at his presence.

'Look, come and look, I've got hair.' She spoke with innocent babyish glee, 'Mummy says I'm a big girl now, and look, I get all hot when I rub by here.'

Her small juvenile hand began touching and moving between her legs.

'Go on, show me what you do. Push your fingers in as well. Go on, do it now, show me,' Roy goaded.

She did as he asked, giving a naughty childlike grin as she did so.

'And look I've got big titties. They make me feel funny as well when I touch them and they're all funny and squashy. Look, come and squeeze them.'

But he was too scared to touch her in case she told their parents. But he didn't need to touch her; it was all too much for Roy anyway. He unzipped his trousers and, there and then, brought himself to climax.

'You mustn't tell anyone what you did, must you? They'll say you're a naughty, nasty girl. You wouldn't like that, would you?'

'No, I wouldn't' she said emphatically, 'I'm a good girl I am.'

'Of course you are, but it's OK if you show me what you do and let me watch again on another day, OK?'

She nodded her head vigorously in agreement, and he left the room still shaking with the excitement, and with the horrendous apprehension of his parents finding out.

*

His shopping done, Mike headed to the other end of town to collect the children. He had bought a cheapish silver chain and pendant with a birthday stone, and a book about the Suffragette movement – she liked history books, and he was well-pleased with his afternoon's work. And he had used his chequebook for the first time and it made him feel pretty smart and affluent. He got to the school early and so sat in the car browsing through one of his library books and smoking his American ciggy. Amongst the books he had selected this time was a science fiction novel. He liked an occasional one of these because the stories were so unpredictable, and the futuristic gadgets sounded so wonderful. For instance, in this case, there was a description of a machine that could cook food in seconds just by shooting some sort of electric waves at it. He thought Jan would really like one of those. The other was a book called *The Psychology of Love*, from which he hoped he might learn something to help him sort out his life.

As he relaxed, browsing through the sci-fi novel, he occasionally glanced up at the school looking for signs of children, and a memory returned out of the blue, as they often do. He remembered back to his own time in school, not that he was there much in his early years. He had been a sickly child and missed a lot of classtime. At one time, on returning to class after a bout of illness, he had missed the learning of the three-times table. The female teacher, a Miss Lucas, whom he could still see dressed in the knitted green woollen dress, well it looked knitted to him, that she seemed to wear every day, and had hairy warty things on her face, made him go into the class of younger children. There, he had to stand in front of the class and ask them to tell him the answer. Little wonder he was left with a fear of all things mathematical until he got the job at the factory, where numeracy was important and the use of a slide rule for speedy calculations, essential.

He didn't get very far into his book before children spilled out of school like a swarm of angry wasps, darting here and there in a rush to reach waiting parents. The wasps seemed even more buzzy than usual and were no doubt fired up with Christmas fever.

His two were soon with him and they set off home. As usual, they had much to say, well David did. School to Mandy was still a bit of a mystery and the highlight of her day was what they had to eat.

'Dad, look at this.'

David thrust a drawing at Mike who, with due deference to his son's laboured artistry, praised it greatly.

'Did you do a drawing as well, sweetheart?' Mike asked, not wanting to leave Mandy out of the verbal prize-giving.

'I lost mine,' she murmured absent mindedly. 'We had custard for dinner,' she added enthusiastically.

'Well, you can't draw custard, can you?' Mike said, attempting one of his jokes again.

Mandy looked at him blankly, but David chortled with glee.

Jan was already in the kitchen when they got back, and David set about retelling the custard joke, which pleased Mike as it wasn't often he had such success. Janice tittered dutifully at her son's obvious joy as she continued preparing the meal.

'How was your arm today, it's not hurting, is it?' Jan asked with motherly concern.

'Look, my friends have been writing and drawing on the plaster stuff,' David replied, confirming that there obviously wasn't a problem with it.

'Um, very nice too, darling, and where's your drawing, Mandy?'

Mandy shrugged her shoulders with indifference, and asked when Father Christmas was coming.

'Won't be long now, sweetheart. Why don't you go and

153

see if you can do me a nice drawing of Santa,' and the cherubs pranced away to their play table chanting, 'Soon be Christmas, soon be Christmas.'

She turned her attention to Mike, who was picking at the uncooked carrots and crunching them loudly with great enjoyment.

'By the way, I'm working again tonight, OK.'

She didn't even ask if he minded, and Mike just nodded his agreement. He didn't bother to ask her what time she would be back. He didn't want to think about it. She had done one other evening stint since the late night, and was back home at about 11.00 p.m. But that didn't mean she wasn't seeing anyone. And what about when I'm in work, what is she up to then? he wondered.

What Mike didn't know was that Janice wasn't actually thinking actively about meeting Alan that night, or anyone else for that matter. If she did, then fine, if not fine again. She could take it or leave it. After all she still had her own ways. But she was now so much stronger within herself and more sure of who she was. Her character had not been built upon being desired by men, unlike some of her friends who always had to have a man chasing them in order to feel 'feminine', and could not function without them. In fact, all they ever talked about was men, make-up and the like, or their kids if they had any, all which Jan found boring. She wanted to be a person not just a woman, and being a wife and mother made it all the more difficult just to be a person. She didn't consciously think this, that wasn't her way. In fact, trying to sort such issues she found almost painful, and depressing. It was more sort of instinctive. However, person or woman, there was still the problem of sex. And more frequently than ever the idle thought of what a bloody nuisance it was would come into her head.

It was midnight, and she was late again. He had gone to bed at his usual time but hadn't slept. He just lay there, his brain, as usual, working overtime. He had got up once or twice to smoke a cigarette, which didn't really help to calm him down. Despite trying to be rational and sophisticated, and balancing her behaviour with what he had been doing with Babs, he was still struggling with his emotions. His idea of their behaviour being special and sophisticated and modern was fading. It wasn't working as he had hoped. In fact, their marriage seemed to be coming to the end of the line. She must be having a real affair otherwise she would surely say something. If she would only just say that there wasn't anything important, anything serious, going on. In those hours of darkness waiting for her return, his thoughts became as dark as the night outside. This couldn't go on. He enjoyed his time with Babs although he couldn't say he loved her. The sex was great, but is that love? He wasn't sure how this worked any more. Of course, there were other women and if he did leave Jan then he might find someone else apart from Babs. Of course, he could just live on his own, but what a terrible idea. He didn't like that thought one bit.

Jan's rejection of him was now so deeply embedded in his mind he couldn't see how they would ever restart their relationship as a normal married couple. He believed that he still spoke and acted towards Jan and the kids in the same way, but Jan was at a distance, and they did so little together now. If she wasn't serving booze then she was rehearsing for the show. The house was finished so they didn't have that to work at as a team, and they rarely sat together simply watching the telly. Money was not a big issue, because with the benefit of the pay rise they were doing OK financially. But how would it work if they parted? He couldn't be without the children and he certainly wouldn't want to be the one to upset their wonderful happy little lives. And then there were the parents. What would they say? They would be really upset. Christ, what a mess.

155

But something must be done and soon, we cannot continue like this.

He was particularly disappointed at Jan's lateness because they had planned to take the little angels to see Santa in his grotto. They needed to set off early to make certain they saw and did everything they wanted to do. He didn't want to be tearing around the place in a rush. After all, children move slowly, and time doesn't. In order to avoid a sleepless night they hadn't told the kiddies of their plan, so it wouldn't be a huge problem if they left it until another day. But time was getting short and suitable days even shorter.

12.45 a.m. and he heard the front door opening. Thank God she's back, perhaps I'll get some sleep now. Mike turned away from where Jan would soon lie, and tried to sleep.

Next morning Janice was up before Mike and preparing herself for the day out.

Through half-closed eyes he watched her getting dressed. To him she was still extremely desirable and looking at her without her knowing, made his viewing seem very sexy – like watching a stranger through a window. Somehow she sensed he was awake and the moment was lost.

'Time to get up, Mike. We are still going, I take it?'

She spoke quite curtly, but that was normal as she wasn't at her best early in the morning, but he prayed the day would be at least nominally happy.

'Yep, of course,' he said cheerfully, getting out of bed.

They both remained silent as they went about washing and deciding what clothes to wear. Each had looked out of the window checking the weather before making their choice. It was dull and dry, but looked cold, not that they would be spending much time in the open air, and the shops would be well heated so very heavy coats and the like wouldn't be needed. The children were awoken with the good news, and once the sleepiness wore off they rushed about the house as though their shoes were on fire. It was going to be a very tiring day.

The streets were packed with busy shoppers and neither Jan nor Mike really liked crowded places. It was different for Jan at the pub because she was behind the bar watching the masses rather than being amongst them. But they so rarely went into Aberdod that it was a stimulating though exhausting business, especially at Christmas time, and for the children, who were even less used to crowds, an awesome experience. Not only was the place full of people but the traffic in the High Street, the only through road, was horrendous. Two lanes in each direction were full of slow moving cars lorries, buses and the like, and the exhaust fumes hung in the still December air, but Mike was used to obnoxious smells.

Mike and Jan were not the type of drivers who would wriggle the car into silly places just to be near the shops, and they had parked a little way from the city centre and walked the rest of the way – a very wise plan. The main shopping area was largely composed of tall Victorian and Edwardian edifices and the civic area, museum and county council buildings were much admired. And the whole place lent itself well to traditional Yuletide embellishments and looked quite Dickensian. They were both pleased to see that dotted along the main shopping street were still a few men selling from large battered leather suitcases placed on the pavements. When they themselves had been kids such people were quite common, popping up in all sorts of odd corners offering their goodies. They were now few in number and could only be seen on the busiest of days. Because the city no longer wanted such riff-raff on the streets, they kept close to the doorways or walls of the shops to avoid being spotted by the law.

Mike's mother called them spivs and some of them did look old enough to have been the original wartime black marketeers selling nylon stockings and other hard to get items. Today's offerings were cheap wrapping paper, and toys that fell apart in a day or two, but it was interesting to watch their antics as they tried to attract attention and sell as much as they could before the patrolling bobby would move them on. If Mike saw a policeman strolling in their direction he would hang back waiting to see the bargains being hastily stuffed back into the suitcases and the traders running off in the opposite direction. He considered it all part of the Christmas fun.

'Roy, please, do you think I could some extra money, perhaps, for Christmas things. It's Saturday so I thought we could go . . .'
   Her voice faded away as she saw the look of anger on his face.
   'More money. Do think I'm made of the stuff, you pathetic bitch?'
   Babs nervously persevered.
   'Just for the girls, we have to get them some presents.'
   'The girls, the girls, that's all you bloody well go on about,' he whined, mimicking her voice. 'And you better have something good for dinner for me or I'll remind you who's the sodding boss around here.'

Their usual strategy on these occasions was to visit all their favourite shops first, just in case the children's stamina faded away, then have something to eat, then do all the second favourite stores. This visit was to be no different and with their problems set aside for the sake of the kiddies, they set off in good spirits on their great adventure amongst the glitter, lights and seasonal garlands.

It was 5.30 p.m. when they got back, laden with bits and bobs, to the car. The bargains had been too good to miss and Mike had even persuaded Jan to buy some laver bread from the fresh food stalls in the market hall, a great treat.

Fried with some bacon it was to be a lunchtime special sometime next week. The children themselves were somewhat subdued, mostly due to their little brains suffering from an excess of pleasure. The grottoes had been imaginatively done and the theme of the best one had been, Who Killed Cock Robin? Mike and Jan had thought it a strangely murderous choice for a Christmas grotto but, nevertheless, the crudely animated models had fascinated David and Mandy, which was what the day had really been about.

They had visited Santa, and Mandy had reluctantly sat on his lap to tell him what presents she would like. Luckily, all the things mentioned were those that had already been bought for her. David, although he still believed in Father Christmas, didn't want to talk to Santa – that was for babies.

It had been like old times, and many smiles had been exchanged between Mike and Jan, mostly in response to the children's ohs and ahs. But once back home, the peculiar veil that hung between them, keeping them apart, would come down again.

For now, on the surface anyway, it was all happiness and light. They were still a family. But for how much longer?

16

Monday afternoon, two o'clock and Mike was back in work and the happy Saturday in Aberdod seemed far away. Crow was already at the report desk telephoning some results through to the processing plant.

'Yoh, Mike, heard the latest?' he said replacing the receiver.

'Don't start all that again,' Mike said with a smile in his voice.

'No, really bad news, man.'

'Oh yeah, the kettle's broken, I suppose,' Mike quipped, thinking Crow was messing about as usual.

'No, man, this is for real. Big Bob just told me. He said there are too many on each shift and some of us will have to go. Yeah, I bloody well knew this new shift lark was bad news.'

'Go? Go where?'

Mike was stunned, not believing this could be happening.

'Up the road, man.'

'What, sacked? Bloody hell.'

'Bloody good news just before Christmas 'innit? Give us money with one hand and the sack with the other, bastards.'

More samples clattered their way through the delivery system into the lab, and they both turned from the desk to attend to the work in hand.

The afternoon workload was heavy and it wasn't until

5.00 p.m. that things calmed down and they had time to take a break. Mike was immensely downcast and his face showed it.

'Let's have a break now, Crow, before the next lot arrives.'

Mike's mournful expression was too much for Crow.

'Yeah, right, man,' he said, laughing at Mike's miserable expression. 'Watch that chin, man, it's scraping the floor.'

He laughed again.

Mike refused to be cheered up and didn't respond. Instead, he busied himself boiling the kettle and lighting up a cigarette. He offered one to Crow but he said he'd stick to his British fags. As they sat down, Navy Bill joined them. It's amazing how a boiling kettle attracted the other workmates.

'It true then,' Navy said, 'Big Bob said that letters are coming around in a day or so.'

'Bloody hell,' was all Mike could say, still disbelieving the disastrous turn of events.

'Might not be so bad, though,' Old Navy added, puffing on his pipe. 'The old ones like me will go first. You lot will be OK. Don't worry so much, Mike.'

Mike cheered slightly at this flimsy lifeline and began to relax a little. Drinks were made and snacks consumed, magazines browsed. Old Navy finished his pipe, ceremoniously knocking and scraping out the ash into the ashtray, and returned to his work, leaving Crow and Mike alone.

'Aren't you worried at all, Crow?'

Crow didn't lift his head from his reading.

'I'll probably be leaving anyway. Me and Susan are splitting up.'

It was Mike's turn to give a somewhat nervous laugh.

'Oh yeah that'll be the day.'

'No, serious, man, it's finished.'

Mike stared at Crow, his eyes not really seeing Crow at

all, just an empty space and endless workdays without him, and his jokes. And he hadn't ever known anyone who got divorced so didn't know what to say.

'I'm really sorry, mate.'

'Yeah, well things haven't been good for ages and now she's met this other bloke so, well, that's it. I'm not worried. Her parents never liked me anyway. They're chuffed she's got rid of me. Uh, sod 'um all. I've got relatives in France so I'll probably go there for a bit.'

'Christ, Crow, the place won't be the same without you.'

Crow mumbled something that sounded to Mike like 'yeah ditto' and took the last mouthful of his Mars bar.

Mike was utterly devastated. His grandmother really had something to answer for now. Wasn't it supposed to be just three things in a row? What was going on? Was there a conspiracy afoot to break up his entire world? For the last five weeks or so he had thought that things were more or less on the up and up. But then David breaks his arm, Crow says he's splitting up with Susan and he's going to France, and now people are going to be sacked. This was not bloody good news. And to top it all, Janice stays out half the night, God knows where, and doesn't say a word.

'Better get back to it, I suppose,' Mike said morosely, and with a huge sigh.

As he got up his chair made a tooth-jarring screech as it scraped the floor, the sensation adding to Mike's misery.

'Yep, OK.'

Crow was surprisingly cheerful. It seemed his situation was to his liking.

Mike wondered how soon it would be before he was in the same position.

Now he had got used to the idea, Crow was quite happy at the prospect of being a single man again. He hadn't ever wanted to get married but was pressured by the parents on both sides to 'do the right thing', when Susan became pregnant. Susan's parents had paid the deposit on the house and paid for some furniture. But there hadn't ever been any real affection between him and Susan, and certainly no romantic gestures. He had been to France a number of times and liked the place so was looking forward to being a free agent again. Although he would miss Mike and the gang, he said that he certainly wouldn't miss the factory, or house renovations. No more of that nonsense for him.

He was back home by about 10.30 p.m. and not looking forward to telling Janice about Crow or the job losses. He hung up his coat and went into the sitting room, where the gas fire was burning and the room was warm and peaceful. Jan had put up a lot of the Christmas decorations and all that remained was for Mike to get a tree so that Jan could dress that as well. The television was on and Jan was sitting doing some hand sewing and watching the programme at the same time. It seemed a great shame to spoil the homely atmosphere with unpleasant news.

'Hello, have you had a busy shift?' Jan said breezily, mistaking his worried expression for fatigue.

'Not too bad.' He flopped down in the chair opposite her and lit up a fag. 'Decs look good. You've been busy.'

'The kids were driving me mad so I thought I'd get on with it. Just need the tree now. Mr 'Hitler' Brown, as you call him, is getting some in tomorrow. I'll see what they're like.'

'OK, that would be easier than getting one from town.'

'Anyway, are you ready for your supper? It's fish pie. Do you want it in here on a tray?' Jan said, laying down her sewing.

'Yeah, sounds great. Thanks, love.'

He hadn't said, "love", for a long time and saying it

163

seemed a bit odd to his ears. But, yes, he would have liked some warm cuddly comfort, or at least sympathy, for all the bad news he had to tell.

Jan simply said, 'OK,' and went to the kitchen to see to the food.

While he waited for his meal he wondered which bit of news to relate first. He supposed it didn't really matter, though perhaps the work thing first. That would be the issue that affected them most.

'Here we are,' she said, placing the tray on his lap. 'I'll get your coffee in a minute. I want to see the end of this play.'

'Yeah, fine. This smells good.'

Jan didn't reply and took up her sewing again and Mike concentrated on his food, leaving the news until later.

Jan's reaction to both pieces of news was surprisingly unemotional and non-committal, for which Mike was grateful. In a way her calmness helped him to be calmer and more optimistic as well. As far as the problem of work was concerned, they both agreed that Old Navy was probably right and that Mike's job would be safe and, in any case, he could always get another job.

But she was a little more concerned about poor old Crow and Susan, wondering as indeed did Mike, as to how their little daughter would cope without a dad.

'He never talks about Cindy to me at work. I don't think he spends much time with her.'

'God, I can imagine Susan telling him to get out. You know how strong-willed she is.'

'Yeah, and loud,' Mike added.

'She is a bit,' Jan agreed.

'I'll miss Crow in work, though,' Mike said sadly.

'I expect you will, he's been your big mate.'

And that was that. Janice didn't ask what was the actual reason for separating, not that Mike knew. Perhaps she didn't want to get into a discussion about anything too close to their own situation.

It was a day later, after Mike's morning shift, that his grandmother gave him trouble number five. Perhaps she couldn't count.

Janice was out at rehearsals. With seven days to Christmas Eve it was to be the last until the New Year. The show itself was scheduled for the end of January, so Janice would be out rehearsing really hard that month. He had got the children to bed, but not without a struggle, and he had given the *John and Janet* lesson a miss and read them another of their favourites, *Bleep and Booster*. Their Christmas fever was running a temperature and they took some settling. Eventually, he was sitting himself down by the warmly hissing gas fire, with a book and the radio happily chatting to itself in the background. He had only put it on for company; the room seemed too quiet otherwise. A tree had been bought and dressed and stood proudly in the corner of the room, so the house was ready for the big day. As a reward for his babysitting, Mike had treated himself to a whisky and American dry from the Christmas stocks – and one of his Yankee fags.

As he sipped his drink his mind wandered over this and that and work featured large.

The letters about the job losses had been sent to all the workers but only asked for volunteers over a certain age. So Mike was in the clear – for now, maybe. But Crow had decided to go, anyway, just to get his hands on the severance pay. He would miss him a hell of lot when the sad day came. But until then he convinced himself things weren't so bad and everything in the garden was pretty if not lovely. Well, not really, obviously there was still the stand-off between him and Jan, and whatever she was up to on those late nights. And not only that, he still wasn't getting enough real sex for his appetite and was still giving himself a

165

frequent private helping hand, and would have liked to see Julie again. Perhaps he would meet a willing female at the am dram Christmas shindig. Although, he pondered, that's not quite how it should work, is it?

Surely wife swapping should be amongst married people you know. As Pete the Sparky would say, 'Safer innit, mate?' But he had decided for now that he would shut down all these amorous thoughts and concentrate on Christmas celebrations with Jan, the kids, and the rest of the family, although keeping Barbara and sex in general out of his mind was proving very difficult. Added to that, he still hoped Jan's big surprise would lead to a resumption of normal service, as it were, between them.

He slumped back in the easy chair and opened the book, took a swig of his drink, and let out a relaxing sigh. There was a knocking at the front door. He wondered who the hell it could be. He opened the door. It was Barbara, shivering with the cold and tears streaming down her face. She was totally inadequately dressed for a cold night, wearing just her usual skirt and jumper.

'Babs? What a surprise. Come in, come in. You're freezing. What's the matter, why I you crying? Where's Roy, is he with you? Shouldn't he be away, working?' Mike enquired, peering out into the street.

'I'm on my own. I've walked here. We had a row and I don't want to go back. I want to leave him.'

She cried harder than ever and her words were mixed with choking sobs.

'You've what? You walked all that way without a coat?' Mike said, disbelieving that two couples he knew could be in the same state in the same week.

His mind rapidly went up a gear or two, from relaxed to controlled panic. He didn't like being under this sort of pressure and tried not directly to respond to what she was saying. The last thing he wanted was Roy turning up here

166

to smack him on the nose. Bloody hell, perhaps he doesn't know what we've been up to. Or does he? Is that what the row was about?

Has she been saying something silly to Roy, like wanting to live with me? Closing the front door, he pushed her into the room towards the fire.

'Get by the fire, get warm, for Gods sake.'

He pulled an easy chair closer to the heat.

'I didn't know where to go I didn't want to go to my mother's place.'

'Where are the kids?'

'With Roy, at home. He's been working in Aberdod most of the week.'

Thank God, Mike thought, he can't come here and leave the kids alone. Her shoulders began to heave and another wave of sobbing ensued. She didn't seem to have a handkerchief. Mike ran upstairs to fetch one, handing it to her and putting his arm around her shoulders. She looked absolutely exhausted and bedraggled.

'Are you warmer now? You'll feel better in a minute.'

Mike spoke softly, desperately wanting to calm her.

'Yes, I'm feeling a bit better already,' she sniffed, dabbing her eyes and pulling her fingers through her hair in an attempt to tidy it.

'I'll go and make some coffee, that will warm you up.'

In the kitchen, Mike's mind was racing in top gear. Wondering what to do. If Jan found her here there would be an almighty row. Why had she come here, anyway? Surely her parents' place would be the best? Perhaps she thinks she can stay here, Christ, no chance of that. Does she think she and I are going to get together? He wasn't ready for anything like that yet. It had only been a possibility not a certainty. We might, but I'm not ready to make a decision like that. What the hell shall I do? What a mess.

Thank God Jan is out.

'Here we are, hot coffee.'

Mike placed the steaming mug beside her.

'You're so nice to me, Mike. I'm sorry to be like this.'

'That's OK. What the hell has happened? You'll have to go back. What about the children? You can't leave them.'

'I can't talk about it.'

Her eyes began to fill again and Mike moved over to her chair and knelt in front of her, ostensibly to give a simple comforting kiss. He didn't like seeing her in such a state and he was really sorry to see it. She had other ideas, putting her arms around his neck and kissing him hard on the mouth. He remained on his knees but now his body was between her legs. Mike, with a mixture of sympathy and arousal, returned the kiss and lifted her skirt to her waist. Babs gave a moan of consent and expectation, pushing her body closer to the edge of the chair. He pulled her knickers aside as he unzipped his trousers. She groaned loudly as he slipped easily inside her, kissing him passionately and moving her body in rhythm with his. It was soon over.

Mike returned to his chair and felt bad, really bad. He that hollow dragging feeling again and was utterly dismayed at his weakness, because now, how would he get her out of the house, because that is what he had to do, and as quickly and as nicely as possible. Time was racing on and Jan would be home soon. God, what if she had been here tonight? His mouth was speaking to Bab's but his head was saying something else. He couldn't see an easy way out of this problem. To put it crudely, he was up shit creek without a paddle.

Babs continued to sip at her coffee and Mike had lit up a cigarette and finished off his whisky. This is not what he had planned for the evening. And what of his promise to himself about forgetting about sex for Christmas. Slowly and painfully the conversation, such as it was, ground to a halt. Babs had realised that Mike wasn't willing or able to commit himself to either taking her in, or at the least making some move to help her in a more long-term way. She felt isolated and a little dirty. Her marriage vows, which she had taken so seriously, had once again been broken.

'I'd better get back I suppose,' she said sadly, slowly putting the empty mug onto the low table, 'in case the girls wake up and wonder where I am.'

Mike was overjoyed and relieved that she had made her own decision to leave. He was even more relieved that she hadn't said anything about living with him and the like. But he did feel guilty about the way he was treating her and rushing her out of the house back into the cold. But what could he do?

'That's the best idea, Babs, I'm sure you'll sort it out and I'll come and see you as soon as I can, yeah? OK? Look, here's ten bob. Get a taxi, don't walk all that way back.'

He pushed the ten-shilling note into her hand and closed her fingers around it. Christ, I'm treating her like a whore.

'I wish we had that bloody telephone fitted. We could get a taxi from here then.'

She said nothing and began walking towards the door.

'Have you got any change, for the phone? For the taxi?'

She shook her head; she had no handbag or pockets so it wasn't possible for her to have anything with her. He reached into his pockets again.

'Here's some change, there's a phone box by the garage. OK? And don't worry, I'm sure you'll make it up with Roy.'

She looked so pathetic, so dejected, he kissed her lightly on the cheek.

She nodded her head, said nothing, and slowly walked out into the night.

The rehearsals were going well. At least the cast thought so, but, as usual, Bill wanted perfection. It was nearly 10.00 p.m. but he wanted one more run-through of the main theme song. Jan's throat was becoming a little hoarse but

Bill had to be obeyed. In their break time, he did allow a break, Julie had more or less insisted that Jan and Mike go over to their place to a small Christmas party. Jan thought that it sounded a safe situation, having other people around, so had agreed. She hoped she had done the right thing because she didn't like the idea of being alone with Tony. But she suspected that Mike wouldn't mind being with Julie again.

At 10.30 p.m. Bill called it a night and the hall quickly emptied and Jan drove home.

'That Bill keeps you lot at it, doesn't he? You must be shattered with all that singing.'

'Shall I make you a cuppa?'

Mike's guilt over the Bab's business earlier in the evening was making him very solicitous towards Jan.

'That would be nice. Have the kids been good for you?'

'Yeah, eventually. They're really excited about Christmas, as usual.'

'And what have you been up to?' Jan asked innocently enough.

But Mike became a little flustered.

'Oh nothing much, I read for a bit, and listened to the radio,' he said, a little too pointedly, but thankfully, Jan didn't notice.

'Julie's having a party on Saturday, I've said we'll go. Is that OK?'

'Yeah, funny day to have a party, three days before Christmas Eve.'

'Well, don't forget they don't have any kids so their Christmas is quiet.'

'Suppose so.'

Mike didn't know whether to be pleased or not. What about his quiet Christmas?

'Right, I'll make that drink now. What do you fancy? Tea?'

'Please,' Jan replied distractedly as she browsed a magazine and lit up a cigarette.

'You bitch, I'll teach you to bloody well run out on me, you cow.'

He grabbed her by the hair, smacking her hard across the face. Barbara gave a groan of pain. He hit her again, letting go of her hair, and she stumbled across the room, bumping into the arm of the sofa and falling to the floor.

'Get up, get up now, you sodding stupid whore.'

'Please don't hit me again, please.'

'Shut your mouth, turn around bitch, bend over that chair. Do it, for Christ's sake, now.'

'Not again, no please don't.'

'Shut up.' He hit her across the back of her head. 'I'm going to give you your favourite.'

He tore her knickers off, leaving red weals on her skin.

'Not that, Roy, not there. Please, it hurts me.'

'Too bloody bad, slut.'

She gave a stifled screech of pain.

17

As they lay in bed that night, together but apart, each were thinking over the day's events. Janice's head was still singing songs from the show, but the invitation from Julie, which Janice had been trying to avoid, had reminded her of her time not only with Tony, but also with Alan. She didn't count the couple of very brief fumbles with Ken, the leading man in the show. That had been a situation which she and countless other women were familiar with and would normally extricate themselves from with ease. But Jan, in her new 'wife-swapping' mode, had allowed his flirting to go a little further than normal just to see what would happen and had now pushed that particular minor event to the back of her memory. She was confused and couldn't really comprehend how her life over the last six weeks or so had taken the turn it had. She didn't like the way their lives were running on half lies. Well, not even lies exactly, but simply the silence. They hardly talked to each other. She was waiting for something to change. If the flow of their lives altered to a different direction, she would follow. In matters such as these she was not, as yet, an instigator.

Jan was thinking that her times with Alan and Tony were a time-consuming effort that she really didn't need to make. She had relented and seen Tony again for one afternoon at his house. He was a charmer and could be very persuasive, particularly when his beseeching was mixed with his sense of humour. She couldn't deny to herself that her time with both Alan and Tony had been exhilarating, but she could get this at home, either by herself or maybe with Mike, if they both made a huge effort to sort their problems out. Of course, it would have to come from Mike, because there would be a limit on what she said to him as she considered it was imperative to keep her special secret – as an escape route.

Mike was equally confused but his thoughts were initially of a more sensual encounter. His body, and his mind, for that is where 99 per cent of sexual pleasure is, was still reliving his time with Babs that very evening. But the incident had left him feeling very alone, isolated somehow, maybe because there was no one he could talk to about his thoughts. But he was beginning to believe that sex with Babs or Julie or, if it came to that, with any other 'swap' was great because it had no responisiblity. It was exciting because it was like being on a perpetual honeymoon, without the marriage. But this spell could be broken if, as happened tonight, it became burdened with responsibility and sadness. That was not what he wanted. He wanted pleasure all the way. But was it possible to carry on like this forever, just taking the good bits with other women and shunning the bad moments the problems, another individual's problem? He liked her, he liked her a lot. She seemed so gentle and vulnerable and if he and Jan did break up then Babs would be his first choice. He felt he had been an absolute bastard for not actively helping her some way, and for taking advantage of her as he had. And he decided he would like to give her a little present, hopefully to see her smile again, and made his mind up to do just that and to hell with the consequences. But after that relatively light-hearted thought his mind soon went back to its more serious considerations.

It now seemed to him that to her sex was love, and when

she said the other day at her house 'come to bed to love me' she must have meant just that. She expressed her affection, her love for someone, by allowing such intimacy. Is that how women should be? Is that indeed how all women are? But people aren't all the same and it must all be a question of degree, and the variables mind-warpingly complex. But it was certainly how he viewed Jan's sexual rejection of him. In his eyes she had fallen out of love with him. If this scenario was indeed how love and sex worked then he wished there was a much much clearer dividing line. When is a kiss between a man and a woman sexual and when not? It's a physical act after all. If it's possible to have sex without love and why is it called lovemaking? Do I still love Jan in the same way without sex? Mike's head wrestled with the puzzle. If only there could be a logical plan in black and white that everyone could follow. That way everyone would know exactly what to expect and how to behave – but wouldn't life be boring?

The next morning, Thursday, was Mike's last shift before his Christmas holidays and would be the only day before Christmas that he could try and see Babs. Firstly, because he assumed Roy would have lots of days off from his high powered job and might be at home when he called, and, secondly, David and Mandy were breaking up from school that very day, and from tomorrow would need entertaining at home. Apart from all that, at sometime he had to see his neighbour, Keith, about moving the piano. He was going to be busy. His idea for the day was that he would pop into Baray after his morning shift to buy a small gift for Babs, deliver it, then home, and then see Keith.

Mike had sworn to himself that he would not weaken from his resolve this time and wouldn't go to bed with her. It wouldn't be easy though, because just thinking about her aroused him a lot and gave him a nice feeling inside. Was that love, or sex? Whichever it was he wanted the festive season over before making any decisions about his marriage and Babs. Of course, the dismal possibility was still with him that Jan might be making plans along similar lines.

Turning the car into the now familiar approach to Roy's place, Mike wasn't feeling so blasé about giving a gift to Babs. The bravado of his bedtime analysis last night was waning. Now in daylight, albeit grey and overcast, his actions seemed very rash and if Jan found out, could result in her making her choice about their marriage all the sooner, something he didn't want to be responsible for. And the other thing was how would Barbara explain the gift? She would have to keep the present secret or say she bought it for herself. Overall, he was undecided whether he should give it or not. But he still wanted to see her anyway, to make sure she was all right.

He rang the doorbell, his other hand in his pocket clutching the gift of a small brooch.

'Do you live here sir?'

Mike started at the voice behind him; he turned to see that it came from a young policeman coming out of his hiding place at the side of the porch, stamping out his illicit cigarette underfoot as he did so. He gave Mike an odd look, as though he knew him.

'No, just visiting.'

'Who would that be then?'

'Roy Jameson, top flat.'

'And who are you then, Sir?'

He opened his notebook, pen poised. What the hell was going on?

'Mike Jones. Has there been a robbery or something?' Mike asked, thinking about all those antiques in Roy's flat, although burglary was a rare event in the town.

'And your address, sir?' the constable asked, ignoring his question.

Mike gave his address and began to feel very uncomfortable, as though he had done something wrong. This visit was supposed to be discreet. Fat chance of that now.

'Do you know the occupants well, sir?'

'Well, yes. Roy used to work with me, and I know his wife, a little,' he lied, not wishing to implicate himself in any way; he certainly couldn't say anything else.

'There's been a bit of an accident. It looks as though Mrs Jameson took too many pills and I'm afraid she's dead.'

Dead, how can she be dead? He looked vacantly at the constable who was watching him closely.

'Are you all right, Mr Jones?'

'Yeah, yes. I'm OK. 'Are you sure its Ba . . . I mean, are you sure it's Mrs Jameson?'

'Yes, I'm afraid so?'

'What about her . . . Roy . . . husband?'

'Oh, he's all right. Quite cheerful really, but that could be a reaction to the shock I suppose. But he doesn't want any visitors. That's why I'm here. He's with the children now. Two nice little girls. Shame, isn't it?'

'Yes, yes it is.'

He spoke softly, then turned and started to walk to the car.

'The inspector will probably want to talk to you at some time, Mr Jones. He will be talking to everyone who knew her, just to make sure it was an accident.'

Mike said nothing and continued walking away, shoulders hunched and his head bowed as though in reverence to Babs. The tiny gift in his pocket felt as heavy as lead and he wanted rid of it. Before getting back into the car he walked slowly to the edge of the old harbour where the grey-coloured tide was half-heartedly slapping the harbour wall. He took the package from his coat pocket, looked at it briefly and then threw it as far out as he could into the murky waters.

'Bye Babs, see you sometime,' he murmured to himself.

He sat in the car just staring ahead, smoking a cigarette, his brain beginning to work again. Dead, Babs dead. It doesn't seem real. Christ, what a terrible thing to happen, I would go crazy if it was Jan. And what did he mean, 'make sure it was an accident?' I know she had a row with Roy, but surely she wouldn't have killed herself over a bit of a tiff. And the girls, she doted on those kids. His compassionate nature gave him a feeling of sadness but there was no great sense of loss and he was ashamed to realise that he was glad that the Babs' business was over. He probably wouldn't have ever stopped seeing her of his own volition because when it came to sex his resolve was very weak. But now he felt relieved somehow, free. But what was he to do now? And what the hell was he to tell Jan? Yes, he might be free of Babs but there were still complications. What if the police ask when I last saw her? If I tell the truth, Jan will know she was in our house the other night. Not that she seems to care what I do, but I do care.

The whole incident was like something from a television play and he drove home in a daze. Even talking to a policeman was a first for him and he found it hard to believe what had happened, and the nearer he got to home the more unreal the situation seemed. Mike began to experience that odd hollow feeling of vulnerability and uncertainty, which most of us have at some time during our lives. A desire to escape to a safe haven, to return to the primeval cave and to think of nothing at all. Just be away from everyone and everything. Sadly for Mike, this wasn't possible. His life was full and complicated and his mind refused to shut up. Instead, it repeated all his thoughts again.

Was it an accident or did she commit suicide? And, most importantly of all, why?

Thank God it was nothing to do with me. But one thing he did have clear in his mind was that he would, sex or no sex, go all out to sort things with Janice. He had already begun to realise that he had developed an entirely selfish attitude to sex and women in general. The whole business had really been an ego-boosting exercise and his own satisfaction paramount. Perhaps his theories on the subject had been far too biological, believing that women existed just for sex. And although his sexual appetite remained, he was going to put more emphasis on love, although his nature wouldn't allow him to use the word lightly, and he intended putting some study into the subject. But at least his theorising wouldn't involve him with women.

When he got home Jan was in the kitchen.

'You're late Mike, it's 3.00 p.m. – problems at work?'

'No, work was fine.'

'You haven't heard the news then?' she said, sounding a bit like Crow starting one of his revelations.

'News? What news?'

'Barbara, Roy's wife, she's dead. Julie reckons she took an overdose of something.'

'God, that's awful, Jan.'

How did she know? He tried to sound concerned, and as though it was news to him too.

'Apparently Babs's mother found her this morning and rang Julie to see if she knew where Roy was working. And I saw Jules for a few minutes in town lunchtime and she told me. Isn't it awful? Why did she do such a terrible thing? And those poor little girls left with him.'

Once again she emphasised the 'him'. And that was that. The brevity of Jan's comments belied the depth of her concern and she was as caring as Mike. Her quiet, rather phlegmatic relaxed nature was one of the traits that had attracted him to her in the first place, and had been a brake upon his high speed, high tension, and quick-reaction character.

'Do want something to eat?' she continued.

178

'No, I'm OK. I had something in work. I'll have a cuppa though.'

'OK, I'll get it in a minute. Why are you so late?' she asked innocently, as she ran some water into the kettle.

Mike thought lying was the better part of deceit and had the brainwave of evoking the buying of Christmas presents as a cover, knowing that Jan wouldn't question it.

'Well, I had a few secret jobs to do.'

Jan carried on with her chores and didn't directly look at him, which made it easier for him to lie. He had got good at lying and it was something else that would have to stop.

'Oh, lovely,' Jan said with surprising good humour.

What he would do if, or when, the police arrived to talk to him, was best left until it happened. However, he really couldn't believe his luck. Jan bumping into Jules had been a godsend, saving him from making a difficult explanation.

'Don't forget we're going to Julie's on Saturday night.'

'Yeah, OK, Darl,' Mike replied with far less enthusiasm than the previous visit, but did remember to start saying Darl, again.

He had to begin somewhere with his new policy believing that if he kept repeating niceties then Jan might get the message. The party itself should be a safe situation as regards sex. There would be quite a crowd, he hoped, just in case he weakened in his pledge not to go to bed with Julie. Of course, she might not want to go with him, but that possibility didn't cross his mind.

'Is it Rita's turn to fetch the kids or ours?'

'She should be here soon. They'll be full of it today, last day of school today.'

'Kettle's ready, I'll make your coffee.'

He still had to see Keith when he got home from work at 5.00 p.m., but Mike couldn't see a problem. He was a friendly bloke – and strong. After all, the piano was rather heavy. Mike sat at the dining table with his coffee and a

Yankee fag, looking through the day's post, mostly Christmas cards. It was his job to arrange the cards on the silver-sprayed beech tree branch propped on the cupboard next to the now empty fish tank. And that was another thing he intended reinstating after Christmas was over. The branch idea was something they had seen years ago in a television programme about Christmas time in the countryside and liked the idea. The branch came from their favourite country spot, and its gathering was another seasonal task for Mike, which he enjoyed greatly.

'Oh, yeah, I went to the main post office when I was in town today, about the phone. They said they would call after Christmas to look at the job. But it will have to be a party line with next door.'

'God, sharing with nosey old Mrs Hill, great.'

The Hills were not his favourite neighbours, not since he had watched Mrs Hill adding to Mike's DIY mess in the rear garden by throwing her rubbish over the fence. She also liked to watch who was calling at the house by spying from behind her curtains. By contrast, her husband was a timid little chap who wouldn't say good morning to a hamster.

'Well, it will be better than nothing, and we could have our own line eventually.'

'Yeah, I suppose so.'

Suddenly excited banging on the front door broke the quiet.

'Here they come,' Jan said, heading for the door. 'Are you ready for our little darlings?' she called, with mock exasperation from the hallway, but really she was happy to see them.

'Mummy, Daddy,' Mandy stormed in waving at Jan her offering of her handmade Christmas card.

David too had a similar present and Janice sat at the table studying their astounding works of craftsmanship with immense pleasure. From his chair at the opposite side of the table, Mike watched the children milling around their mother – his wife. It gave him a pleasant warm feeling in his gut, and in his eyes it was a lovely family scene and a huge contrast to the sadness of that very morning across the other side of town. But the world rolls on, regardless. However, it was an idyllic domestic vision, and it reinforced his determination for change. He hoped that it was not too late.

18

Saturday night was once again party night. The kiddies had been deposited with Mike's mum, although according to a passing remark from Janice, they probably wouldn't be staying the night, a statement which Mike with his new philosophy on his sexual behaviour, only too readily and wordlessly accepted but why she had come to this conclusion eluded him. Ablutions were attended to just as thoroughly, just in case something naughty did occur. And on this occasion Jan's preparations were distinctly less elaborate and her choice of clothes much quicker. She didn't ever use a lot of make-up, but even that task was completed at speed, with a slick of lipstick and a dab of this and that. The stockings and suspender belt were disappointedly absent, but nevertheless, he enjoyed watching her dress – as much as he did watching her undress. The bedroom atmosphere was far more relaxed than the last time they headed in Julie's direction. Mike knew why he was relaxed about the evening, but not why Jan was. Could it be Tony was the one she had been seeing, and now familiarity had bred contempt? In the sense that their relationship was now so well established, that she didn't need to dress up to make him interested in her.

Busy with her dressing and hair, Jan was actually choosing what to wear with just as much care as last time they went to Julie's, but for a different reason. I think I'll wear tights just in case Tony's hands should wander, but there shouldn't be a problem tonight. There will be too many people about for him to try anything on. I still like him, but not like that anymore, and he tries too hard to impress me all the time. He's a bit too much of a smoothie. Nice hands though. I know, I'll wear the dress that shows my cleavage off. Bit of a tease but I don't want to be too plain, do I? She inwardly smiled at her thoughts. How she had changed. So confident.'

'You look great.'

It was something Mike hadn't said for a long time. He spoke rather tentatively and quietly, not wishing to engender any aggravation.

Jan didn't respond directly in any way, so he added, 'Ready to go?'

'I'm ready,' she said, giving him a little smile, and checking herself over once again in the mirror.

Mike was thrilled by just that simple smile and thought there was an ember of hope for them after all. But he intended treading very cautiously indeed.

Mike considered that parties could sometimes have a knack of announcing their presence without any obvious advertising. And as they approached Julie's, the house gave out a distinct aura of expectancy, though nothing could actually be seen. Mike thought that perhaps there was some subliminal energy source from the hosts that he could detect. All these fanciful ideas and he hadn't even had a drink – yet.

'Hi, Jan, Hi, Mike. Haven't seen you for ages, you naughty boy. Why haven't you called to see me? You're nice and early. We can have a natter. Like your dress, Jan,' Jules said, taking their coats and ushering them into the large living room, empty of people, but the record player was blasting out her Tom Jones' favourite, "Delilah".

The room was tidier than he remembered it. The piles of

books that had stood here and there had been returned to their shelves and festive baubles, balloons and bunting festooned the room. And some of the furniture had been moved back against the walls to give an open space for dancing.

'Did you make it or buy it? God, I wish I had breasts like yours.'

Julie was in her usual breathless high-speed speaking mode and not really bothering to wait for answers.

'No, made it. It's nothing special.'

Jan ignored the breast comment, as she did most of what Julie said for much of the time.

'You're too modest, Jan. Isn't she Mike? I couldn't make something like that. Help yourself to a drink, Mike, you know you can do anything here.'

She giggled, and gave him a knowing look with her beautiful blue eyes.

She was wearing a white mini-dress, which accentuated the colour of her eyes and hair, and he wondered lustfully if she was still wearing panties with days of the week on them. Her remark about not calling on her made him think what chances he had missed. He hadn't thought that there would have been any opportunities to see her because she and Tony worked the same hours – unlike Roy and Babs. He could feel his resolve weakening and he took a deep breath, letting it out slowly in an attempt to damp down his sexual thoughts and regret at the loss of sexual adventures with Julie. Backing away from them, and the dress discussions, he headed for the drinks' table, depositing a contribution of that infamous sherry from-the-wood they liked, but actually choosing a whisky and American for himself.

'Oh, I'll have one as well, please, Mike. What about you, Jan?'

Before choices could be made Tony bounded into the room, full of fun.

184

'Hello, gorgeous,' he said, walking in and looking towards Mike, then turning and adding, 'and Jan, of course.'

Gathering Jan in his arms, he gave her a big dramatic back-bending kiss, cupping a breast with one hand as he did so.

'Crikey, Tony, let a girl breathe, will you?' Jan said cheerfully, when he eventually released her.

The mood was light-hearted and they all laughed at Tony's welcome. But Mike's viscera, or was it his heartstrings, gave a lurch of disillusionment. Was Tony the one she had been seeing? They seemed so familiar with each other. He could be the one.

Does Jan want to stay the night? I thought this was going to be a sex-free night. Well bugger it, I'm sticking to it; I don't want to slide back into this swapping stuff again. I want normality.

'Mike, what about those drinks?' Julie's voice broke through his despondency.

'Uh, oh yeah. Tony's award-winning performance put me off for a minute.'

They all thought this was a marvellous piece of repartee and laughed at his unintentional wit.

It wasn't long before other optimistic revellers began arriving, searching for fun, and alcohol. There were some guests that Mike didn't know but most he did. Pete the Sparky turned up with his latest conquest, and, of course, Bill the am dram supremo, together with his wife. She was rarely seen except at the bigger parties, which this seemed to be turning into. Jules obviously didn't do things by halves. Marie was there with her shotgun idol, and another chap who for some reason had come dressed as a woman, complete with wig, make-up, high heels, the lot. This caused quite a stir, which surprised Mike. He thought these actor types would be used to such extrovert behaviour, but it certainly added to the party atmosphere. The only person that he hadn't seen turn up was Roy. But under the circumstances Mike hadn't expected to see him, for which he was thankful. Very soon the house was filled with laughter, music and cigarette smoke, as the booze continued its good works.

Mike was playing a very low-key game and trying to avoid Julie, which wasn't difficult in the crowd. Janice, with her very low tolerance to drink, was talking away nineteen to the dozen as she went from group to group and looked in her element. She had chosen a middling short black dress; she said she was too fat for a mini-dress, which showed off her glorious, smooth white cleavage which Julie, and others, had admired so much. He spent some watching her face as she talked, her head bobbing or shaking in agreement – or not, her perfect teeth shining white against red lips. She looked lovely. If only she could be so chatty when she was sober perhaps they could then sort out their lives, Mike thought rather bitterly. He was back into his dull, 'I hate parties' mood, and his optimism was at low ebb. He had even been thinking about the lay-offs at work, perhaps even his own, and the loss of his mate, Crow. All had crossed his mind, hardly the stuff of an entertaining night out. It seemed the death of Barbara was having a bigger effect on him than he realised, and in his more observational role, looking at the crowd around him, the whole business seemed a mindless search for enjoyment and a thorough waste of time.

'Hey, Mike, over here.'

Pete and Tony were waving frantically from across the room.

Mike hadn't drunk very much and was struggling to be just a bit cheerful and sociable, and so reluctantly crossed the room, putting on a forced smile as he did so.

'Come on, in here.'

Tony spoke as though he had a big secret. He almost pushed Mike and Pete along the hall passage and into a small room used as a general storage area, complete with vacuum cleaner, mop and bucket and other household necessities.

On an old-fashioned wooden planked table stood an eight-millimetre cine-projector. Its gleaming metal and chrome finish looked out of place amongst the junk. And on the opposite wall an old white bed sheet had been rigged to act as a screen.

'What's all this about, Tone?' Mike asked unnecessarily, as he had already guessed what was planned.

'I've borrowed this from a mate at work and Roy's bringing some films and stuff over. You know, blue films. Should spice the place up a bit, eh?' Tony replied with great enthusiasm, rubbing his hands together and grinning widely.

Mike wondered if this was a first for Tony. Mike had seen so many at work that he was a rather blasé about the prospect.

'Roy's coming here tonight after what happened with his wife?'

Mike couldn't believe that even Roy could be so indifferent and callous.

'Oh, yeah, well, he's only dropping them off, he won't be staying. Well, I shouldn't think so anyway.' Tony sounded a little bit guilty, but was still grinning.

'Anyway it's no good hanging about the house on his own without a woman, is it?' Pete said, giving Mike a knowing wink and adding, ''Ere, have a fag and cheer up, for God's sake. Its a party innit, and it's Christmas.'

'What I thought was that we'd set it up in here then people can come in groups. Good idea, yeah?'

'Oh, yeah, bloody marvellous,' Mike said in a tone of mock admiration.

What he really thought was that he wished he had stayed at home. He wasn't in the mood for this, or for seeing Roy.

'Don't forget, Tony, tell 'um when they're watching they've got to keep their hands in view, not in their pockets.'

Pete laughed, and took a long drag on his fag.

When Mike returned to the other room, many people had already spilled out, as they do, from the core of the party into the hall, stairway and kitchen. He found Janice in the kitchen nibbling titbits and talking and laughing with a young-looking bloke who Mike thought he recognised from somewhere.

'Where have you been?' Jan said with a smile. And what are you up to with Tony and Pete?'

'Me? Nothing. It's Tony and Pete messing about. I think I'll have another drink.'

'This is Alan, by the way,' Jan said, looking closely at Mike as though expecting some reaction.

'Hello, mate, are you another actor?'

They both laughed, which made Mike feel a bit foolish and very insigificant.

'No, I'm a policeman.'

Shit, that's it. He's that young copper who was at Bab's place. I thought I'd seen him before. What is he doing here? Perhaps he's a friend of Tony. He looks different without his uniform. Mike prayed he wouldn't say anything about seeing him at Babs that day, not that it really mattered anymore.

'Oh, right, sorry, I think I'll go and get that drink.'

He moved quickly away and headed for the drinks. He needed more drink to get him in the party mood. He was here, so he had to make the best of it.

As it happened, Janice had asked Alan to come to the party without saying anything to Julie or Tony. Jan had suggested if he turned up when the festivities were under way, then no one would even notice him coming in. And no one had. She thought it would be a novel idea to be out in public with Alan. After all, it was Christmas, and she felt sorry for him. He was working over the holidays so this was to be his taste of Yuletide joy.

It must have been about 11.45 p.m. when he saw Roy pushing his way through the crowded entrance hall, carrying a small cardboard box. He seemed to know where he was going and made his way to the improvised cinema, and Mike remembered from the conversation in the lab that he must have been here before, although without the success with Jules that Mike had enjoyed. He hadn't seen Roy for a while and wasn't looking forward to seeing him now. His wife had died only a few days ago and the funeral hadn't taken place yet. How the hell could he possibly be out at a party?

Mike found it unbelievable.

'Hi, Mike, long time no see.'

Mike was at the drinks table downing yet another one. He had definitely made up for lost time and was now approaching his limit.

'Didn't expect to see you here, Roy, after what happened. I'm really sorry . . .'

Roy cut him short, gave a sort of wave of his hand and responded cheerfully, speaking with his usual quiet quivering voice.

'Not to worry, get the funeral out of the way on Monday and things will soon get back to normal. I've got a couple of birds in mind. Shan't be on my own for long. Got to get my rations regular, haven't I, eh?' He gave one of his ugly sneers. 'Anyway, I'm here on a special mission. Tony wanted some films so I brought some over.'

He leered towards one of the dancing women, adjusting his specs over his nose.

'Look at the arse on that one, fantastic.'

Mike was amazed at Roy's behaviour. In a way he was grateful that he wasn't all weepy and sad, but not that he was so bloody cheerful and lewd – as usual. He was even

189

more astounded when Roy turned his back to the crowd, reached into his coat pocket and took out a bundle of photos.

'Bet you haven't seen these, have you? Tony and Pete have. Here, look at these.'

He started handing them to Mike one by one. Some were naked shots of women he didn't know, but then he was handed photos of Babs in far more explicit poses. In one of these, with legs spread, she was holding herself wide apart. In another she was holding a Cola bottle by the neck with the other end deep inside her. She looked utterly sad and immensely pathetic.

'Good, eh?' he sneered. 'Yeah, right up her love tunnel.'

Mike exploded. His fist rose from his side, took a wide slow-motion arc and landed with a crunch on the side of Roy's face. Mike winched with pain as his knuckles crashed into that leering, supercilious grin.

Roy staggered, his hands flailing the air, trying to reach hold of an invisible rope, missing it, and falling heavily to the floor, the drinks, table rattling with the impact.

The room fell silent, apart from one or two people who, thinking Roy was drunk, laughed with knowing and joyous sympathy. The music and distant voices in the 'cine room' and hallway continued, acting as a buffer to the embarrassing quietness. Jan pushed through the gathering. The expression on her face was a mixture of embarrassment and shock. Mike's actions were so out of character. What was the matter with him? Why did he do such a thing?

Someone began helping Roy to his feet, another recovered his spectacles, handing them to him. Mike discreetly and quickly picked up a couple of the photos that had dropped from Roy's hand in the fracas and shoved them in his own pocket out of sight. He was already regretting what he had done and felt extremely self-conscious at causing such a scene. But he simply couldn't take any more of Roy's slimy innuendoes about Barbara. It was true that he hadn't ever punched anyone before, and it was nothing like he expected. In films it looked so easy and painless, well, painless to the giver, but Mike's hand hurt like hell and he tried to massage away the discomfort.

Tony, obviously tipped off by someone, dashed into the room looking concerned.

'What the hell happened, Mike?'

'He's had too much to drink, Tony. I'm really sorry. I'll take him home,' Jan answered for Mike, for which he was immensely grateful.

'No need to go, love, get some coffee down him. He'll be all right. How about you Roy? Are you OK?' Tony asked, turning to Roy who was now on his feet and busy tidying himself up.

'Yeah, I'll live.'

The party noises had started up again and people dispersed and carried on unconcernedly.

'We won't stay, Tony. It's best if we go, it's getting late anyway. Thank Jules for us and I'll see her at drama after Christmas. OK?'

'What ever you say, princess. Merry Christmas.'

Tony looked relieved at the prospect of them leaving, and gave Jan a peck on the cheek.

'Merry Christmas.'

They stepped outside into a world far removed from the aggravations and tensions of the evening. It was snowing. The soft cold flakes touching warm skin was a pleasant distraction for them both, but neither of them spoke. The streets were wonderfully hushed and white, and they would normally have enjoyed the prospect of this Christmas-card weather. However, the mood in the car was cold and sombre. Mike was still nursing his hand and feeling utterly stupid and forlorn. He was ashamed with himself for acting as he had and would have preferred to have a less than perfect evening at the party rather than this ignominious departure. Christ, what would his grandmother have thought of this? It had been very much 'a bit of the unnecessary'.

Jan said nothing but was formulating, with an effort, what she should say to him. She couldn't just let such an unusual occurrence go by without an explaination. She had been enjoying the party and now wondered what people would be saying about them behind their back. But then she reasoned Roy wasn't popular at the am dram so perhaps the comments, if any, wouldn't be so bad.

Back home, Jan turned on the gas fire in the sitting room and insisted he should bathe his injured hand and then a drink of coffee. Mike slumped in a chair, absorbing the warmth of the fire, feeling safe and protected from the disagreeable evening.

However, without the children sleeping upstairs, the house seemed unpleasantly still and quiet, which added to his sense of isolation.

'Here, get this down you. You'll feel better soon.'

She put the coffee down on the low table next to him. Her voice had a curt, scolding edge to it as though he had been a naughty boy.

'Let me look at your hand.'

She took his hand, pressing it here and there to see if there was any obvious damage.

'Does that hurt?'

'No, not really. It's feeling better, anyway.'

'I bet it will be bruised tomorrow. What made you do such a thing Mike? I thought you were his mate.'

'He wasn't my mate, as you call him. It was just, well . . .'

Mike was finding an honest explanation difficult as to why he had tolerated Roy, and how involved he had become with Babs. He took a deep breath.

'It was what he was saying about Babs – Barbara. And these photos he was showing me tonight.'

He took the pictures that Roy had dropped from his pocket and handed them to Jan.

Jan looked at them with a degree of disbelief, disgust and excitment; excited by the sexual content and, disgusted by the fact that Roy, her husband, would show them around to other people.

'What an awful thing to do to her, showing things like this about the place. What if she were still alive and found out? It's really awful. I always said he was creepy and horrible.'

Listening to Jan agreeing with him, and recalling his times with Babs, and the shame of his actions, Mike's sympathetic emotions mixed with his sadness and disappointment of his life with Jan, welled up within him. His eyes filled with tears.

Jan looked across at him.

'Mike, what's the matter? What's wrong?'

Mike sobbed.

'He shouldn't have done that, showing those photos, treating her like that,' he cried.

Jan sat staring at him. What was the matter with him? This isn't the Mike she knew. A thought struck her like a rock.

She said quietly and slowly, not sure whether she wanted an answer, 'Were you in love with her?'

'God no, not like you mean, anyway. I felt sorry for her that's all,' he sobbed.

Jan breathed a sigh of relief. She was grateful that the inner core of their relationship hadn't been compromised, as their sex life had. She hadn't any loving feelings for Alan or Tony and had considered the relationships as totally peripheral events in her life. But she didn't make a move to comfort him. To her, that didn't seem quite the right thing to do. Why should she provide succour to him over another woman, albeit a dead one? Yet, deep down, she was crying a little too and was pleased he still had his compassion, even though in their hectic lives over the past months she hadn't thought too much about such virtues. But now, more than ever, she wasn't really sure what Mike wanted from life. Would he have left her for Babara? Did he want to be single again, like Crow?

'I knew something like this would happen,' Jan said in 'I told you so' tone. 'You get too involved.' She paused. 'I only did it because I thought that's what you wanted me to do.' She paused again, adding in a quiet voice, 'Do you want us to split up?'

'God, Jan, no. Of course not. I don't want that. It was all for sex 'cos, you know, you and me haven't been, well, you know, doing anything together – in bed.'

He spoke hesitantly, bad memories of past discussions returning, and he knew he was moving onto dangerous ground and he didn't want a shouting match. But despite feeling stupid and in a weak position to question Jan about her 'friends', they were nevertheless talking. And Mike saw, through his muddled and unhappy state, an opportunity to assess Jan's involvement with, well, whoever it was she had been seeing. He had to know. He dried his eyes with his large white handkerchief and let out a big sigh.

'And what about you? You've been seeing someone. Is it Tony? Do you want us to split up?' he asked defensively, returning her own question.

'Me? Tony? No. If you must know it was Alan – the policeman you saw tonight.'

Jan's attitudes to her experiences were, had been, of a different nature from Mike's. Her adventures had been outside her – just play-acting. And she didn't like the way this was going. She didn't want to talk about herself. But

194

she did want some return to normality and if talking like this would help that aim, then she was willing to make some effort.

A wave of relief swept over Mike. He almost wanted to laugh. Alan, that young copper – that's it. He was the one I saw at Babs' house that day she died. Bloody hell, him. He really couldn't see Janice wanting to live with him.

'Drink up, let's get some sleep. We've got to pick the kids up in the morning,' Jan said in an uncharacteristic business-like manner, taking control of the situation and bringing any deeper discussions to an end – for the time being at least.

Mike, feeling even sillier and inadequate, willingly agreed, pleased that a line had been drawn under the farcical events of the party, and, as far as he was concerned, under the Barbara and Julie business as well.

Jan didn't fully realise it but she had gained a lot from her adventurous sexual play-time. Her confidence as a person and as a woman had grown stronger. She had learnt that men varied in their sexual preference too. Alan, for instance, sometimes liked to watch her touching herself, while he did the same, which, of course, suited her needs as well. And Tony preferred her to be on top, something she hadn't tried before. All this new information had given her the idea that men weren't all the same and some, like Alan, weren't very confident and 'masculine'. And if men varied sexually, then perhaps so did women. All of which had made her think that she might not be such an oddity after all.

19

The very instant he opened his eyes vivid memories erupted into his mental view. The catastrophic party, Barbara's death, the loss of his best friend, Crow, the changes at work, all flashed before his eyes like the proverbial drowning man, and all the pictures depressed him greatly. It seemed that nothing had turned out as he had hoped and everything was a bloody awful mess. All his reading and amateur analysis of love and sex hadn't really made anything any clearer to him. Most of the books he'd dragged out of the library said that sex and love were totally integrated and that was that, which Mike could not believe. Certainly, there had to be a thread of common regard, otherwise it would be mindless rape or pure mechanical sexual release. It was complicated but he had broken it all down to the fact that, logically, both parties had to feel secure with each other, for however a brief a time, for it to be possible to indulge in the act itself. After all, just showing each other's naked body needs a confident state of mind.

Love, he had decided, was more of an academic nature in which higher applied civilised attitudes came to the fore, such as compassion and concern for another person in which the loss of that person or that person's reciprocated love would lead to the loss of all those other factors – confidence, security and stuff like that. And all these differing intellectual ethics and needs varied in degree and in interpretation between different people. We are all totally isolated as individuals, and, in life and love, compromise is the only way to retain, to gain, some degree of personal satisfaction of our desires. It seemed to him it was a case of intellect versus primitive biology, and complicated with it, and how intellect, love, could be equated with the human desire to bang away like dogs, eluded him. In any event, despite their short chat last night, there seemed a long way to go, and ideas such as these were not something Janice would be interested in discussing. In any case, who the hell lives their lives consciously thinking and philosophising? And his theories didn't seem of any practical use.

He had awoken to find himself alone in bed, which made his depression even deeper. He liked to be up and about with or before Jan and the kids, otherwise it felt as though he was still on shift work. And another old familiar, the sad void in his gut, was back. His confidence had taken a beating and his present mood of pessimism led him on to think that after his behaviour last night, and despite the clearing of the air between them, he had now totally lost Jan's love as it used to be and the outlook for them was bleak. And they still hadn't actually said that they still loved each other, nor touched each other. It was obvious there was to be no big romantic reconciliation and that it was going to be a long uphill slog to regain how they used to be, if ever. And yet there must still be a trace of the deep friendliness, he couldn't think how else to describe it, still existing between them. They had shared so many of each other's interests and personal moods of sadness and happiness. That surely they had gained a larger understanding of themselves and the world around them. If only each of them could realise the fact that now, perhaps, sex and romanticism were not the glue that held them together but some, as yet indefinable, element of unselfish concern.

For Mike even the imminent Yuletide celebrations and

Jan's huge surprise present did nothing to alleviate his mood. Having all these miserable ideas was a shame because the Sunday-morning world outside was a winter wonderland and the drab grey street transformed and shining white in the sunlight. Jan, concerned that the weather might take a turn for the worse, had braved the snow-covered roads and collected the kids from his mother's, the sheer weight of their much derided old car being a great help in sloshing through the whiteness. But hearing the children back home in the house surprised him, as Jan normally wouldn't drive if there were the slightest hint of ice, snow, or fog – not like her at all.

Downstairs, Mandy and David were nagging Jan to let them loose outside and then he heard the children on the stairs and braced himself for the onslaught.

'Dad, come and help us build a snowman.'

'Oh, yes, Daddy. Will you? And is Father Christmas coming today on his sleigh 'cos it's been snowing. Is he Dad?'

Mandy, bursting with excitement and joy, screeched hysterically and leapt on the bed, literally shaking Mike out of his reverie.

'Not today but he'll be here soon.'

'Will you help us, Dad – pleeese?' David pleaded again.

'OK, OK, but can I have some breakfast first?'

They dashed away whooping with pleasure and simultaneously Jan and Mike shouted after them, 'Be careful on those stairs.'

The last thing Mike and Jan wanted was another trip to the hospital with broken bones.

'Mum, Mum, Dad's going to help us,' David said, with obvious pride that his father was such a good sport.

'Mum, can I take Blackie out to see the snow?' Mandy said, already scooping up the dozing puss and heading for the door.

'I don't think he'll like it, sweetheart,' Jan replied, smiling broadly at the enthusiastic antics of her offspring.

But Mandy was not so easily dissuaded and went outside and deposited the cat onto the snow-covered garden. She watched Blackie's reaction with an almost sadistic grin on her face. The cat shook his paws with absolute distaste, and, giving Mandy a look of great malevolence, ran quickly between her legs back into the house. Little girls of angelic appearance can be so very evil.

Between dressing the kids in warm clothes, Jan busied herself with getting Mike's and her own breakfast. The children had already had theirs at grandma's so that was one less job for her to do. Mike came into the dining room with a rather sheepish expression on his face. He was still feeling self-conscious and silly over the Roy business and sat down quietly at the table trying to be invisible.

'Will you want toast after your cereal, Mike?' Jan called from the kitchen.

'Yes, please – and marmalade, please.'

'OK.'

Jan soon returned with hot toast and coffee and Mike soon began to feel a little more real.

'Kids couldn't wait then?'

'No, they're having a great time but it's cold out there and I bet they'll be in soon.'

'You were brave,' Mike said, giving Jan a little smile of admiration, 'driving out in the snow.'

'Was I? I just thought it might snow again, thought I'd get it over with.'

The truth was that Jan had startled herself by realising that if she wanted too she could take more control of their lives and make decisions. She really didn't want these new self-imposed responsibilities because she had been reasonably content with the situation up until the wife-swapping saga. And even though she was just as sensitive and sympathetic as Mike, her inner self was kept safely inside her. It was as though the outside world was filtered, levelled out somehow through this outer shell, protecting her from violent swings of opinion and emotions one way or the other. But Mike was not so lucky and took everything face on and hated letting go of people and situations. But for Jan, and all that stuff with Alan and Tony she could easily do without, and to her it wouldn't be a loss.

It now seemed to her, that she was in general doing more analysing than she ever had, and that Mike was not as strong as she always had thought. The other world of his sexuality and sex with other women appeared to have weakened his resolve and his forward-looking nature. He had wallowed in sensual thoughts and actions. Of course, it didn't enter her head that her own more secretive sex life might have any influence on their marriage. Perhaps, she thought, the extra income and the comparative security of his job were to blame as well. Had it made him mentally lazy? He hadn't bothered with his hobbies for ages. The fish tank was still empty, and he hadn't yet finished the garden. It occurred to Jan that with Christmas on the doorstep and the New Year chasing close behind, it would be a good time for a radical change in their lives – perhaps far away from Baray.

Breakfast over, Mike got up from the table stubbing out his first cigarette of the day and headed for the coat rack.

'Well, I'd better get out there and build the snowman.'

'OK, love,' Jan said sympathetically. 'Rather you than me,' she said cheerfully, 'and I'll get on with the veg for dinner, and Marion gave me some fresh brussels sprouts from the garden. I thought we'd have pork chops today. Is that all right?'

'Yum, yum,' said Mike with genuine enthusiasm, and smiled broadly to himself – she called me 'love'.

As Mike worked with the children creating their frozen

masterpiece, his mind was often elsewhere working through, yet again, his problems and ideas. The question uppermost in his mind, now that he was fully awake, was how would he and Keith get the piano along the street tomorrow night in the snow? It wouldn't be a good idea to get it wet, as he was sure it would damage it in some way. And he could hardly clear a pathway to the old shop could he? That would be a shade obvious. He would just have to hope the snow would clear by Christmas Eve.

His other problem was should he go to Babs' funeral tomorrow. The police hadn't ever called on him and he assumed they were satisfied it was suicide after all. Christ, what else could it be? Had they thought Roy had murdered her? Bloody hell, surely not even Roy could do that. Still, it was all sorted very quickly, and no inquest. Perhaps the police wanted it over by Christmas, which Mike supposed was better for her children, but what sort of life they would have without her, God knows. No, on reflection it wouldn't be a good idea to go, and, in any case, Jan was working at the hotel and he would have to look after the kids. His conclusion pleased him because he really didn't want anything more to do with Roy.

'Dad, can we have a carrot for his nose?'

'I should think so, son, go and ask your mother.'

'Dad, my hands are cold and hurting,' moaned Mandy.

'Well, you can go indoors now if you like, sweetheart. We've nearly finished and you can see him from the window.'

Mandy trotted off mournfully indoors, leaving David and Mike to put the finishing touches to the snowman. Jan joined them, bringing a couple of huge black buttons for its eyes and an old woollen scarf.

'There we go, he won't feel the cold so much now,' Jan said, tying the scarf around its icy neck.

David, not used to his mother making jokey remarks, tittered, 'You say funny things, Mum, just like Dad.'

'Well, I can be just as silly if I try really hard, you know,' Jan said with a little laugh and added, 'Come on, you lot, time for elevenses.'

20

Christmas Eve and all was well, well, almost. Mike still had to get the piano in the house somehow after Jan had gone to bed. As it happened, most people up and down the street had swept the snow from their bit of pavement outside their houses so Mike had gone out and done the same. The way was clear for the great adventure. Jan was at work serving the partying hordes at the hotel and the children were strangely quiet. Mike hoped that perhaps they had burned themselves out with excited anticipation, but from past experience he knew that as evening approached they would come to life with a vengeance. He had contacted Keith, his neighbour, and he had said he would be in all night so when Mike was ready for the move so was he. Mr 'Hitler' Brown had given Mike the key to the old shop earlier that day and it had been burning a hole in his pocket ever since. In a way, his worry over getting the piano into the house was spoiling his Christmas and Mike wanted it over with. He just hoped it was all going to be worth the effort – and expense.

Mike was feeling much better today and he thought Janice seemed pretty cheerful as well. Christmas time for Mike tended to be a time of mixed emotions anyway, even without the trauma of fisticuffs. His father had been terminally ill at Christmas and had died early in the January and it had been a deeply miserable time for Marion, Mike and his mother. All of which made this time of year especially poignant, particularly for his mother who always made certain that his father was not forgotten and would make some pointed remark or other. Thankfully, having the children around totally diluted what had the potential for being a very miserable time. Jan and Mike enjoyed Christmas Eve best of all. The excitement of the kiddies was massively infectious and they got almost as excited as they did. To help get them to bed and to tire them out, they usually took them for a walk in the evening to the town centre to look at the decorations and the tree. But with all the snow around they might have to think of something else. Something else they had done for the last few years was calling in on Crow and Susan sometime during the day for a little drink and chat. This year, with Crow and Susan splitting up, they were going to give it a miss. In any case, Jan would be at the hotel until 3.00 p.m. and they had left it too late to call anyway.

It was about midnight when Jan was at last satisfied that the kids' presents were sorted and arranged in the right unpacking order. She didn't want batteries to surface before the toy itself, and similar unnecessary concerns. For the main present they had decided to splash out with the extra money from work and get Mandy and David, bicycles. David had wanted a bike for ages but had no idea he was to get one. Mandy, too, was having a smaller version with stabilisers because, although she hadn't actually asked for one, no doubt she would have when David went zooming up and down the lane behind the house.

Mike was getting concerned that Keith would be in bed by the time it was safe to move the piano and so fussed around trying to encourage Janice to finish up and get to bed. The house and the street in general were very quiet. The skies had cleared and outside the snow had frozen hard, but all the households along the terrace had cleared the snow outside their own houses during the day, so luckily Mike had didn't have to make any excuses to Jan as to why he had done the same. But it was still amazing good luck that the weather was dry and the pavements clear.

'Right, I'm done. Up we go. You carry David's stuff and I'll take Mandy's.'

Mike had had a few drinks that evening whilst watching Jan doing her sorting and was in a cheerful mood. He stumbled up the first couple of stairs and began giggling.

'And be quiet,' Jan scolded.

Once upstairs, they crept about placing the bulging pillowcases beside the sleeping cherubs, with Mike still trying to suppress his giggles.

'Don't forget to drink the sherry and eat the mince pie, Father Christmas.'

'What, more booze? I like Christmas,' Mike whispered drunkenly, spluttering bits of pie everywhere and choking on his suppressed mirth. Jan too was by now so amused by Mike's antics she began giggling as well.

'Here have some pie and sherry,' Mike croaked, his eyes shining with the hilarity of the situation.

'Shush, we'll wake them.'

'Drink up, love, it's Christmas' Mike said, swigging his glass empty.

Drinks and pies consumed, they tiptoed along the landing to their bedroom, shutting the door and then burst out laughing.

'And whose idea was that?' Mike said.

'Guess who? Your mother. The kids wanted me to do it, for Father Christmas.'

'Well, it was good for a laugh anyway.'

Their eyes met and for once the animosity in their glances had been replaced with a softer happier, more relaxed gaze. They both seemed to recognise this fact simultaneously, and stopped laughing and talking and for what seemed a long time, but wasn't, just looked at each other. In different circumstances this aura of warmth emanating from them both could have lead, well, to something even more intimate. It was the moment he longed for. But, as with so many other precious moments in life, it wasn't at the right time. Mike had something special to do and he dispelled the moment by announcing, with a flash of his old inventiveness, that he wasn't sure he had locked up the car properly and would just pop out to see if it was OK. It was a story not completely unfamiliar to Jan; he often double-checked the car at night. She just smiled and said it was late and that the children would be awake at dawn, if not before, and that sleep was the priority.

Mike loped down the stairs, fuelled with the energy of the alcohol, along the street and knocked very quietly at Keith's and Rita's door.

'Sorry I'm so late, mate, got a bit delayed.'

'That's OK, Mike. Let's give it a go, shall we? I've had a couple of drinks, mind you.'

'That makes two of us.'

They both laughed quietly, each recognising they were both in the same state.

The street was silent. There was no moon but the sky was clear and starry and they walked to the shop talking in whispers.

'Bloody cold out here, Mike.'

' 'Tis a bit,' Mike agreed, rubbing his hands together.

Unlocking the door, they groped about in the dark shop trying to locate the piano.

Mike could feel the giggles coming on again and Keith wasn't much better. Mike bumped into something.

'I think this is it, feels like it anyway. Funny how we can lose something that big,' Mike said.

'As the actress said to the bishop,' Keith retorted.

That was it. They both choked hysterically on their stifled laughter.

'Hey, I just thought. What if the cops come by while were in here messing about?' Keith said, still choking on his laughter.

They both went into even more violent spasms of absolute fun.

'Oh, God,' said Keith, wiping the tears from his eyes, 'let's shift this dammed thing before we get arrested.'

To which they once more went into fits of laughter.

Once the piano was in the street and the shop locked behind them, they began half-pushing, half-dragging the blessed thing along the pavement. It was heavier than they had anticipated and, to make matters worse, as it went along over the uneven flagstones of the pavement, the keys tinkled, causing huge amount of laughs.

'Lovely tune, Mike, pity we don't know the words,' Keith joked in a whisper and they both convulsed themselves to a standstill once again.

'We don't want Jan to hear it. We'll have to lift it up off the pavement.'

Eventually the piano was being carried the last few yards up the path and into the sitting room. The exertion of carrying it had sobered them up a little and they were both glad the task was over.

'Thanks, Keith mate, that was great. All in and done.'

'As the actress said to the bishop.'

'Don't start all that again, get out of here.'

'Yeah, see you, Matey.'

By the time Mike had rigged up a crude red bow of crepe paper around the piano and climbed the stairs, Janice was asleep. He slid into bed as quietly as he could, deeply regretting once again that earlier lost moment but expectantly excited at the prospect of the morrow.

'Mum, Dad, Father Christmas has been.'

Mandy leapt on the bed dragging the pillowcase stuffed with gifts onto their bed. Mike and Jan both gave a groan as she landed upon their chests, momentarily taking their breath away.

'Oh God, Jan, it's only six o clock,' said Mike and gave another winded groan as David joined Mandy on the bed.

'Look, look, what I've got,' screamed Mandy, as manic as ever and tearing off packaging at great speed as though her little life depended on it. 'I've got my own *John and Janet* book.'

David took a more measured approach to the whole process and at intervals gave out many 'cors' and 'oos' of surprise and approval. Mike and Jan were soon wide awake and joining in the unpacking fun and there were still the bicycles waiting downstairs – and the piano.

What a day it was going to be.

* * * * *

'Crow, bloody hell. How the hell you doing, mate? Haven't seen you for ages. Come in, come in.'

'Happy New Year, man. How did Christmas go?'

'Really good, yeah great. Things back to normal now. Thank God.'

'Back to normal. What, after Christmas, you mean?'

'Yeah, well, that and me and Jan had a bit of a funny patch ourselves,' Mike answered with momentary uncharacteristic candour.

They had reached the sitting room and sat opposite each other, each on the edge of their seats eager to exchange gossip.

'Jan's out with the kids. Want a drink? There's plenty still here.'

'No, man, it's a bit early. It's only 10.00 a.m. Have you taken to drink or what?' Crow said and laughed.

'It's good to see you, mate. What are you up to now?'

Crow passed Mike a fag and they lit up before he continued.

'Well, I'm off to France soon. I was going before Christmas but I had that bloody Asian flu – it was really bad, man.'

'Yeah, it's everywhere. Some people have died and there's been a few off at work with it. Touch wood, we've been OK – so far.'

'Anyway, I've got a job as a gardener in a big house with English people. Well, garden labourer really. They've got a real gardener already.'

'A gardener? Bloody hell, bit of a change from the factory.'

Crow laughed again.

'Yeah, well, I'll soon learn the weeds from the plants.'

'How the heck did you find that job?'

'From a friend of Susan's. Glad to get me out of the country I expect. It turned out she's got people over there as well and they know someone who knows someone and, well, I got the job. So I'm just doing the rounds, saying goodbye to me mates.'

'We might be on the move ourselves soon.'

'Yeah, man. Where to?'

'Well, we've been thinking of looking for a smallholding in darkest Wales and have a go at farming or something. Well, it was Jan's idea really; mind you it would be great to have a quieter life, be great for the kids too. They're already nagging us about having a dog and rabbits and God knows what.'

'Bloody hell, we'll both be working on the land then. At least you know your cabbages from your rhubarb.'

'Yep, hope so, and don't forget to send me an address and I'll send you ours.'

'Yeah, shall do, mate.'

209

They chatted on for about an hour before Crow said he had to go. Crow said nothing about his divorce so Mike didn't mention it either.

'It's going to be strange without you, Crow,' Mike said sadly.

God only knew when Mike would see him again.

Christmas time had indeed gone well for Mike and Jan, as indeed had the New Year celebrations. The New Year had been especially meaningful and was seen by them both as an end to the events and the roaring pace of the old year. And the piano – that had been a huge success and Jan had laughed and cried with surprise. But he had had a surprise as well. Janice had bought through Rita's mail order club, a new 35 millimetre single-lens reflex camera. Mike had been stunned at Jan's gift and surprised she had thought so much of him to spend so much money. And, yes, it had lead to sex, or was it love?

At the end of an exhausting Christmas Day the children at long last had been settled in bed and Jan and Mike soon followed them up the wooden hill. It had been an exciting encounter, with a hint of nervousness, almost like they were making love for the first time. It had been such a long time since they had been together in that way that, somehow, they really were starting from the beginning. And Mike had remembered all he had learned from his adventures, and in quiet moments he was still rerunning the events in his head.

'Thanks for the camera, Darl, it's fantastic.'

'And thank you for the piano,' she murmured with a smile.

They were lying in bed close together, facing each other, giving and receiving kisses.

'I love you Jan, you know that.'

'You're not so bad yourself,' Jan mumurmed, mischievously.

'Gee thanks. If you're not a good girl Father Christmas will take your present back.'

'I think I'd rather be a naughty girl tonight.'

The warmth and intimacy of the moment was already affecting Mike, and Jan could feel the hardness against her thighs. She, too, was basking in the warm glow of the occasion, and reached down to touch him lightly, a signal that Mike readily responded to, as excited as he was, he remembered all that he had learned and once inside, gently took Jan's hand, placing it between her thighs. Jan eagerly seized upon this wordless recognition of her needs and began touching herself with enthusiasm. Mike moved slowly at first, waiting for Jan to approach her own satisfaction. Jan's moans of pleasure excited Mike even more and soon they were both gasping and groaning with ecstasy and release. All was well with the world . . .

'Get the door, Darl, I'm trying to get these little pests to bed.'

'OK.'

Mike opened to door and peered into the night-time street.

'Hi, Mike,' the familiar tremulous voice said, 'haven't seen you for ages. This is Wendy, my new friend. Can we come in?'